SARANORMAL

A Perfect Storm

by Phoebe Rivers

SIMON SPOTLIGHT
New York   London   Toronto   Sydney   New Delhi

SIMON SPOTLIGHT
An imprint of Simon & Schuster Children's Publishing Division
1230 Avenue of the Americas, New York, New York 10020
Copyright © 2013 by Simon & Schuster, Inc.
All rights reserved, including the right of reproduction in whole or in part in any form.
SIMON SPOTLIGHT and colophon are registered trademarks of Simon & Schuster, Inc.
Text by Sarah Albee
For information about special discounts for bulk purchases, please contact Simon & Schuster Special Sales at 1-866-506-1949 or business@simonandschuster.com.
Manufactured in the United States of America 0913 OFF
First Edition 10 9 8 7 6 5 4 3 2 1
ISBN 978-1-4424-8958-5 (pbk)
ISBN 978-1-4424-8959-2 (hc)
ISBN 978-1-4424-8960-8 (eBook)
Library of Congress Catalog Card Number 2013933228

Chapter 1

"It's only week three of school and already I'm bored with all the guys at Stellamar Middle School," my best friend, Lily, announced as she stirred the pool of butterscotch sauce at the bottom of her sundae glass.

"I know, right?" agreed Avery. She grimaced, her mouth revealing this month's band color, which was bright green. The bands she used for her braces tended to change color from one orthodontist appointment to the next. "That's the problem with living in a small town."

"It's true," sighed Marlee. "All the guys do at lunchtime this year is sit around in big packs talking about sports. They don't pay attention to any of us."

"Except Sara, here," said Avery, pointing at me with her spoon. "They notice you, because you give off that 'I'm not interested' vibe, which of course makes them interested. Can you teach me how to pull that off?"

"She pulls it off because she's actually not interested in any of them," Marlee joked, grinning at me. "Right, Sara? You're not crushing on anyone at school so far this year, right?"

"Earth to Sara," said Miranda, waving a hand back and forth in front of my face.

I jumped. Tried to focus on my friends. Tried to recover and act like I'd been paying attention, when really, I'd been staring out the window at the man standing on the sidewalk. He was dressed in strange clothing, unlike anything anyone else wore these days. Beneath his battered sailor hat I could see long, jet-black hair, loosely tied back in a ponytail. His pants were knee-length, his soiled blue coat fastened with big brass buttons, his thick-soled black shoes topped with large buckles.

Oh, and he shimmered slightly around the edges.

He was a spirit. A spirit I'd seen before, back at my house.

The question was, what was he doing *here*, outside Scoops Ice Cream Parlor? Had he come here to look for me?

Lily nudged me. "You okay?" she asked.

I smiled weakly. "I'm fine," I said. "I guess it's been a long week." But I wasn't that fine. I was having that familiar, unpleasant reaction, the one I thought I'd conquered. The tingling feeling that had started in my left foot was moving up my leg. The air around me had grown thick. The lights had grown dimmer, though I know it didn't seem that way to anyone except me.

My eyes darted toward the window again. The spirit wasn't paying any attention to me. I began to relax a little. Maybe he wasn't here to talk to me. He seemed to be muttering to himself. Rather abruptly, he spun on his heel and marched away, his head down, his hands clasped behind his back. Before he'd gone more than a few paces, he grew transparent. He shimmered for a moment, like a barbecue grill on a hot summer day, and then vanished.

Perhaps I should explain.

You know how kids sometimes talk about how they feel different, that no one understands them, that they just don't feel like they fit in sometimes?

Well, trust me. I win the prize. Because I really *am* different.

I can see spirits. Dead people.

I've seen spirits since I was little. Up until recently, I hadn't told anyone about it, not even my dad. But now he knew. And he'd moved us to this shore town in New Jersey the year before, so we could live in a big, ramshackle Victorian house with Lady Azura, my great-grandmother. She had powers too, and she'd been helping me with my own powers. Which was handy, because her house was filled with spirits.

Only two other people know about my powers. One is a boy named Mason Meyer, the guy I have a crush on, though he doesn't know that. Mason goes to a different school. I had barely seen him since the summer had ended, but we did text a lot.

The other person who knows my secret is Lily. Lily Randazzo, my best friend.

Now, back in the ice-cream shop, she saved me, by directing our friends' attention away from my weird, distracted behavior.

"You guys!" she hissed. "Turn around! Act natural! I just spotted Mason Meyer outside, and he's heading in here and he has a friend with him. A totally gorgeous friend."

The rest of us settled down. We pretended we were engrossed in a deep conversation with one another as we heard the bell of the shop tinkle.

Lily and Avery and Miranda had squished in on one side of the booth and were sitting with their backs to the door, Lily nearest the window. Marlee and I were facing the door, so we had a good view as the two guys came in.

I forgot all about the spirit. My mouth went dry and my palms got wet—but this was what usually happened when I first saw Mason.

He noticed us right away and jerked his chin up in a quick hello gesture, grinning sideways a little. I saw him say something to his friend, and the two ambled toward our booth. I wasn't going to pretend I hadn't seen him. I looked up. Smiled. Felt that familiar sensation I'd been feeling whenever I was in Mason's presence, like electricity crackling through my body. I could feel myself flushing. No doubt my fair skin was turning an embarrassing shade of pink, right up to the roots of my blond hair.

I could feel his green eyes gazing at me. I had to look away quickly. He had that effect on me. Like all my bones had turned to rubber. Instead I looked at Lily.

Lily was blushing. Lily, the world's most extroverted, outgoing, never-at-a-loss-for-words person on earth, appeared to have lost the power to speak.

Still avoiding Mason's gaze, I checked out his friend.

Oh. No wonder.

"This is Calvin," Mason said to us, gesturing to his friend.

"Hey," said Calvin with a shy grin. His voice was deep and smooth.

"Hey," we all murmured back.

Calvin was tall—even a little taller than Mason, who was already taller than most boys our age. His dark-brown hair was short on the sides and a little longer on top, and his eyes were a light shade of hazel. I knew that Lily had a weakness for guys with dark hair and light eyes. Especially ones this cute.

I watched Lily pick up her glass of water and take a big, gasping gulp. I suppressed a smile. She'd already fallen for him.

I'd met Mason during the summer, through a series

of weird coincidences. Lily and her family now owned Buddy, a sweet little dog who used to belong to Mason and his family. I sometimes wondered if Mason and I had been meant to meet each other, and if Buddy had brought us together.

Mason went to a school two towns over, in Harbor Isle. I had no idea what he and Calvin were doing at Scoops right now, since Harbor Isle had plenty of fun places to hang out. Maybe, just maybe, he'd come because he knew this was a place I liked to hang out with my friends? I dared to hope that was why. I also dared to hope he had half as big a crush on me as I did on him.

Avery glanced from me to Mason to Lily to Calvin. She giggled again. "So what brings you guys here?" she asked the boys.

"Just passing by."

"No reason."

Calvin and Mason had answered at the same time.

A movement out the window caught my eye. There was that spirit again. What was he *doing* here? I never saw our "house spirits" anywhere except in our house. This was one of the spirits I rarely saw, and I'd kept my distance from him because he didn't seem very friendly. I had assumed, based on his hat, that he was an old sea captain or sailor or something. The late afternoon light cast his face in shadow, as the sun was setting behind him, so I couldn't see his expression very well. But why would he be outside Scoops?

Once again, he didn't try to get my attention. He didn't even look up at me as he passed by the window. I felt relieved all over again that he wasn't here looking for me, but also really puzzled about what he was doing.

Yeah, the whole thing was weird. Weirder than the usual weird, I mean.

Even though I had been focusing on the spirit, I became aware that an awkward silence was descending on our group. I tore my gaze away from the window. Lily was still clearly unable to speak coherently. Luckily, Miranda stepped up.

"So I heard about your award," she said to Mason.

"What award?" asked Avery.

"People were talking about it in dance class the other day," she explained to us. "Harbor Isle Middle

School had a big 'silly award' competition in honor of their homecoming. Evidently Mason got the Best-Dressed Jock Award, and it was published in the Harbor Isle school newspaper. It just came out today."

"How did you hear about it before the paper came out?" asked Marlee.

"Jody Jenner's in our dance class, and she's on the school paper," said Miranda.

"Did you hear about it too, Lil?" Avery asked, giving her a not-very-subtle *Say something!* look. Lily and Miranda were in the same dance class, so it would make sense if Lily knew about it too.

Lily blinked at her. "What? Oh. Um. What?"

I almost laughed but caught myself at the last minute. She *really* liked Calvin!

"Is that true, bro?" said Calvin, turning on Mason. "I haven't seen the paper yet. That's pretty funny."

"Yeah, hilarious," said Mason through gritted teeth.

I knew how much Mason hated being talked about. He tugged at the neck of his sweatshirt, like it had suddenly grown too tight, and shifted his weight from one foot to the other.

"So how'd the soccer game go yesterday?" I blurted

out, desperate to change the subject for his sake.

"Oh, ah, good," said Mason. "Awesome, actually." He shot me a grateful look.

"So you guys won?" I asked.

"I didn't know you played a fall sport," said Marlee.

"He's the goalkeeper," said Calvin. "But I'm the real reason we win games. I play sweeper, so I save his neck ten times a game."

Lily finally came back to earth long enough to laugh at Calvin's joke. He looked pleased to have gotten a reaction from her.

I thought we'd safely deflected the conversation away from his award. But Miranda refused to let it go. "Yeah, Jody told me all about the article in the school paper," she said. "Jody won an award too—I think she won Coolest Family. Her dad's a famous director. Hey, Mason, maybe that means you and Jody were made for each other!"

I couldn't get mad at Miranda for her comment, because she didn't know about my crush on Mason. But I did sneak a peek at Mason to see how he was responding. He definitely seemed to be blushing. He looked at me, and I quickly looked away.

CRASH!

We all whirled around to look toward the counter. Lily's cousin Dawn Marie, who worked there as an ice-cream scooper, was leaning over the counter and staring at the floor, a shocked look on her face.

A metal container full of spoons had crashed to the floor. Spoons had skittered to all corners of the black-and-white-tiled room.

"That was weird," said Dawn Marie to us. "I was nowhere near those. It's like they just jumped off the counter."

We all hopped up to help collect the spoons.

I was stooping down, trying to collect them with the handles all going the same way, when I felt Mason's arm brush mine. A jolt rippled through my whole body.

"Nice attempt at changing the subject," he murmured out of the side of his mouth as he scooped up a scattered group of spoons.

"Yeah, well, I tried," I murmured back. My hair was falling down across my face, so I hoped the others wouldn't notice our private discussion. Or how much I was now blushing from being so close to Mason.

But a few feet away, I could see that Lily was giving me a Look. A whole bunch of emotions chased one another across her face—interest in the nature of my relationship with Mason, excitement about the fact that Mason had a crush-worthy friend, curious about how the canister of spoons just happened to have done a swan dive off the counter.

There's something else you need to know about Mason. He can move objects with his mind.

Chapter 2

Telekinesis, Lady Azura calls it.

I was the only other kid-aged person who knew about his powers, and I had promised him I wouldn't tell anyone.

Over the summer, he and I had been locked in a closet together by Henry, the ghost of a mischievous little boy who lives in my house and loves to cause problems. Mason has asthma and needed his inhaler really badly, so I had started talking to Henry to try and convince him to let us out. When that didn't work, Mason used his powers to open the door. It was the first time I had ever told someone who wasn't an adult about my powers, and the first time Mason had ever told *anyone* about his. It's not like we would have told each other if we hadn't been in that emergency situation together, but I was kind of glad it happened.

Glad he knew. We were friends now. I just wasn't sure if he thought of me as more than a friend.

We'd just finished collecting all the spoons, and Lily was pushing the container across the counter to Dawn Marie, when the bell on the door tinkled again.

Three girls walked in, girls I'd never seen before.

The tall one in the middle really stood out. She was really pretty. She was dressed like a model—well, that is to say, those pictures in fashion magazines showing models snapped without makeup, their hair casually caught up in a perfectly sloppy bun. I don't know much about fashion—that's Lily's area of expertise—but even I could tell that her outfit was amazing.

"Oh! Hey, Jody!" called Lily.

The tall girl flashed a million-dollar smile, as my dad would describe it. I guessed this was the Jody from dance class that Miranda had mentioned.

"Sorry we're late," said Jody, looking directly at Mason. "Hope you haven't been too bored waiting for us."

Mason glanced quickly at me, then shrugged. "Nah, it's cool," he said.

Before I could decide how jealous I should be feeling, Jody took Mason by the sleeve of his sweatshirt and Calvin by the sleeve of *his* sweatshirt, and pulled the two of them toward a booth in a far corner, away from ours. Her two friends followed in their wake.

"Good to see you again, Lila," she said over her shoulder as the five of them smushed into a too-small-for-five-people booth.

"It's Lily," Lily called back. Then she shrugged. "I should be getting home."

"Me too," we all agreed. We returned to our booth to collect our stuff.

We were barely out the door when Lily blurted out what she'd obviously been dying to know.

"So is Jody going out with Calvin?" she asked Miranda.

I was all ears. I wanted to know what the deal was between Jody and Mason.

As usual, Miranda seemed to be a fountain of information.

"Nope, she's not going out with either of those guys," she said. "I heard from Ellie Kramer, who also goes to Harbor Isle, that Jody's dating a high school freshman."

We all digested this information. Still, Mason and

Calvin had obviously planned to meet Jody and her friends. It wasn't an accidental encounter.

"And also I heard that her dad is a famous, like, *really* famous, television director. And her mom used to be a model. But nowadays she's a photographer, a *famous* one, and her photos have been in galleries and stuff."

I thought about how cool it would be to have a mother who was a famous photographer. My own mother had been a really good photographer, and I had inherited her love for it too. But she'd died having me, so I never knew her. I wondered, if she'd lived, whether she'd be famous like Jody's mom. Her pictures were amazing. I bet she would have been.

When I got home, my dad was still at work, and Lady Azura was in a session with a client. She'd been written about in the newspaper earlier this year, and the news services had picked up the story, so her business had really taken off. I was happy for her. I knew that all the extra money was a good thing, but more importantly, it made her feel good to have a lot of clients. To be helping so many people. But it meant that our afternoons together were less and less regular. She'd been helping me with my powers, teaching me how to deal with different situations and passing on all the wisdom she had from eighty some odd years of dealing with being able to see spirits. I missed getting to spend a lot of time together.

My dad came home soon after I did. As a special treat, he brought home takeout from Thai Taste, my favorite Thai restaurant, and we had a delicious dinner together. I had to do a ton of homework, so I didn't get to bed until after eleven.

I fell asleep quickly and then had the strangest dream.

In my dream, I rose from bed, wearing the actual nightshirt I'd worn to bed in real life—an old T-shirt of my dad's. I walked out of my room, down the hall, and into a room I rarely went into during the daytime. It was the hexagonal-shaped room with pale blue walls. The room that was usually occupied by the spirit of the man in the sailor hat, the one I had seen outside Scoops.

In my dream, it was dark and shadowy, but still daytime, the way it might be in the late afternoon on a drizzly fall day. An old-fashioned clock under a glass dome sat on the mantelpiece, ticking loudly. At first I thought I was alone in the room. And then I saw that there was someone sitting at the writing desk over near the window. A girl. A girl with long blond hair. She was bent over, writing. Not on a computer, though. She was writing with a pen, in a small book that looked like a journal. She didn't look up. I moved closer to her. She was writing so intently a strand of hair had fallen across one eye. Maybe she hadn't seen me.

I cleared my throat. Did it again.

She looked up, startled. As her hair fell away from her face, I saw that it was me. Me, except with longer hair. But I only looked at myself for a split second, because then I woke up with a start.

It was the middle of the night, and the room was freezing. That, too, was weird, because when I'd gone to bed it had been nice and warm in my room. Now, though, it felt icy cold.

I turned on the light next to my bed. The clock said 3:38. I'd kicked the coverlet off the bed entirely. It lay in a heap on the floor. I pulled it back up and around myself, turned out the light, and went back to sleep.

Chapter 3

The next afternoon, Friday at last, Lily and I met after classes were over to walk home. We did this most afternoons. But today we were extra excited because Lily was sleeping over. I used to avoid having Lily over for sleepovers because of all the issues that came with living in a haunted house and trying to hide from your best friend that you could see spirits. But now that Lily knew about my powers—I had told her over the summer—I didn't have to try and hide anything from her.

It was three thirty in the afternoon, the sun still shining, the shadows lengthening. But there was something strange about the light. The sky was a weird, greenish color, and everything seemed sort of backlit, with an eerie glimmer. The day was still warm for the season, but since we'd walked to school that morning, a wind had sprung up. Dry leaves skittered and swirled around us, whipping our hair around our faces.

As usual, Lily had more energy than a normal walking pace could accommodate. She bounced along next to me. Then danced a few steps ahead and spun around to talk to me while walking backward. Then broke into a skip.

Lily never just walked. She was high energy. High enthusiasm. Just fun-loving and extroverted. A good contrast to my shy, avoid-attention, introverted self. We were opposites in so many ways, but we were alike in all the important ways.

"So guess what I brought for the sleepover?" she asked me, her dark eyes shining.

"Stuff to make s'mores?" I guessed.

"Nope. Better."

"A movie we can watch?"

"Nope. I better tell you, because you'll never guess."

"Okay. Tell me."

She spun around again and faced me, skipping backward without either of us having to lose a step.

"A spirit board!" she whispered.

I blinked at her. "A spirit board," I repeated. I knew what one was, of course. One of those board games where you ask a question and then move the pointer and hope a spirit answers yes or no. Or spells out a word to answer it. I'd never actually used one before. Given that Lily knew I had way more than my share of success in communicating with those from the Great Beyond, I felt perplexed by her. Why would she think I'd want to play with a game that supposedly conjured spirits, when I was already surrounded by them?

"Huh. Well, that's nice," I said weakly, because she seemed to expect me to say something. "That explains why you brought such a lumpy overnight bag, I guess."

Her face fell. "You don't like the idea?"

"Well, um, it's not that I don't like the idea," I said. "It's just that, well, it's like suggesting to a mailman that he go for a nice, long walk on his day off."

Lily rolled her eyes. "Come on, Sara. It's time you started looking at your powers as something fun, rather than a burden. What if we conjure up Fred Astaire and Ginger Rogers? They could give us dancing lessons!"

Now it was my turn to roll my eyes. "Come with me to Elber's. My dad gave me money for groceries. You have to help me think of what to make for dinner tonight."

Shopping at Elber's helped distract Lily from the spirit

board idea. We found some baby artichokes and decided to make pasta with them, even though neither of us had ever cooked with fresh artichokes before.

As we stood in line to buy our stuff, Lily texted her mother and asked her how we should prepare them. Mrs. Randazzo can do anything when it comes to food. She's an amazing cook.

Mrs. Randazzo texted Lily back about thirty seconds later with detailed instructions, so Lily had time to run back for lemons and parsley before I'd even finished putting the other stuff on the belt.

When we got to my house, a car was parked out front. That meant Lady Azura had a client. We walked around to the side door leading into the kitchen, so we wouldn't disturb her session.

Soon we had the artichokes cleaned, cut into quarters, and simmering in a saucepan with olive oil, lemon juice, oregano, and garlic. I chopped parsley while Lily demonstrated ballet moves for me.

"This is called a *fondu* combination with a *relevé*," she said, standing with one arm extended to the counter edge and the other curled in an arch over her head.

I had no clue what she was talking about, but she

looked so graceful, even getting up on tippy-toes with her beat-up sneakers.

"Lovely, Lily!" said Lady Azura. She'd entered the kitchen behind us.

Lily twirled across the kitchen and gave her a hug. You'd think they hadn't seen each other in months. I loved that my best friend and my great-grandmother got along so well, though. Lily was Lady Azura's most devoted follower.

"It smells divine," said Lady Azura, moving toward the stove. She lifted the lid on the artichokes, and a cloud of steam rose up, bathing the kitchen in more delicious aromas.

I grinned. "We've called Mrs. Randazzo four times for advice," I said. "Otherwise we would never have thought to pull off the outer leaves and cut the pointy top part away."

"Guess what I brought over, Lady Azura!" said Lily. "A spirit board!" She supplied the answer without waiting for Lady Azura to guess. "But Sara doesn't want to do it." Lily shot me an exasperated look.

I moved to the sink to fill a large pot with water for the pasta. "It's not that," I said. "It's just that I already have a lot of spirits in my life. I don't need any more."

The truth was, while I was relieved that Lily knew about my powers now, and that we could talk about them openly, I just wasn't all that comfortable conjuring up random spirits with my best friend. Spirits were like people, and sometimes they turned out to be really different than you expected. It wasn't something I liked to mess around with. "If you want to meet a spirit, I am more than happy to introduce you to Henry on the third floor. He is, after all, a distant relative of yours."

Henry definitely liked to wreak havoc, as I mentioned before, but he was also pretty cute when he was sitting still and not causing problems. Last fall, when I was just getting to know Lily, she was up in my crafts room with me, and Henry had escaped from his closet. He'd seemed to be drawn to Lily and acted up more than usual when she was around. When I told Lady Azura, she mentioned that Henry was a distant relative of Lily's, and that explained why he'd been drawn to her. It seemed like a fun idea to have them meet. I'd told Lily about him, of course, since telling her about my powers and the spirits that lived in my house. But so far I had not tried to initiate an introduction. Most likely she wouldn't be able to actually *see* him, but it was easy enough to see the chaos he was capable of causing. It might actually be fun.

Lily shook her head. "I want to meet an *exciting* spirit," she said, "not a little kid who has to spend eternity in a supply closet. I want someone who was famous, or in show biz somehow!"

"Henry *is* exciting," I persisted. "Remember how he almost knocked a bookcase over on Jayden at the Halloween party last year?"

I looked to Lady Azura for backup. I was positive she would react with the same lack of enthusiasm I felt. But instead I saw a smile spread across her face. "Delightful idea!" she said.

Lily shot me an *Aha!* look.

"Spirit boards can sometimes be useful conduits to tapping into the spirit realm, so long as they are used responsibly," she said.

"See, Sara? I told you she'd be psyched about it!" taunted Lily. "Even though I am not completely sure what a conduit is," she admitted.

"However—"

Oh, good, I thought. Lady Azura had added a "however."

"However, we certainly don't need a spirit board in this house to contact the dead. If you'd like, after dinner, we can go to my room and have a séance."

Lily grinned and twirled in a circle, doing a little happy dance.

"It's been awhile since I contacted anyone famous, just for fun," Lady Azura mused. "I did once contact Elvis so he could sing 'Love Me Tender' just for me."

Lily looked totally awestruck. I, however, was feeling quite the opposite. One of my English vocab words popped into my head: "apprehensive," and it summed up how I was feeling about this whole plan.

"But doing it just for fun?" I said. "Think about what might happen! What if something goes wrong?"

"I am a professional, Sara," Lady Azura scoffed. "I conduct séances all the time for my clients. It's perfectly harmless."

Just then the door opened, and my dad stepped into the kitchen, bringing with him a swirl of dry leaves. So the matter was forgotten for the moment. But I didn't have a good feeling about the evening.

Chapter 4

The artichoke pasta turned out pretty well. Both my dad and Lady Azura had second helpings. My great-grandmother is a tiny woman. I often wonder where she puts it all.

After the dishes were done, my father sat down at the table to open up his pile of mail, while Lady Azura retired to her bedroom to change out of her flowing dress into something a little more comfortable. Lily and I bustled around, collecting stuff to construct giant ice-cream sundaes for ourselves.

"Oh, I forgot about this," said my dad, staring at a thick, cream-colored card he'd just pulled out of a thick, cream-colored envelope. "I've been invited to a wedding in two weeks. It's a buddy of mine from college named Costi. He's getting remarried. Sara, do you want to come as my date? It should actually be pretty fun. The bride, Lena, is an actress on some TV show, and Costi told me there are a few movie stars on the guest list."

"Awesome!" said Lily.

I smiled. "Sure, Dad. Sounds fun. Do you know what TV show the bride is on?"

My dad scratched his head, like he was trying to remember, and then shrugged. "I don't remember. But it was one I've never heard of." Not that surprising, actually. My dad didn't watch a lot of TV.

Recently I'd been a little worried about my dad. He hadn't gone out on a date in weeks, or at least as far as I knew. He was still a handsome guy, for someone over forty at least, and I was concerned that he wasn't having enough fun. He worked a lot, and when he wasn't working, he was always at home, fixing up the house for Lady Azura or reading one of his mystery novels. I loved to read too, but I didn't think he should be spending all his evenings that way.

My dad headed upstairs early, saying he had a report to work on for Monday morning. Lily and I were just scraping the bottoms of our sundae bowls when Lady Azura emerged, wearing her "comfortable" clothes. For her that meant a lime-green cashmere pullover, harem pants, and high-heeled mule slippers. I marveled at the woman's ability to navigate around furniture in those heels. I'd frequently heard her complain that her old bones were achy, and in fact, I had not seen her climb the stairs to the second floor in all the time I'd lived with her. Yet she walked around the house in fancy shoes with high heels. As with everything else about my great-grandmother, the woman was a bundle of contradictions.

"Are we ready?" she asked us.

Lily and I exchanged looks. Lily's look was excited. Mine was unenthusiastic. Lily had to be perplexed by my attitude in general recently. My reluctance to do the séance. My distracted state at Scoops yesterday. My weird relationship with Mason. She had to be wondering why I couldn't just lighten up.

The thing was, I'd told her I didn't *like*-like Mason, but that wasn't exactly true. When I had told her that, I had been unsure of how I felt about him, so it wasn't as if I had lied exactly. It was just hard for me to explain why I felt like I had such a connection with him, since I couldn't tell her about his powers. Because of our connection, our shared secret, we talked and texted a lot. There was no way I could tell her that I'd gotten to know him really well and that now I was definitely, officially crushing on him. What I didn't know was whether he was crushing on me too. I wished I could ask Lily for advice. She'd helped me out a lot with my first-ever crush, Jayden Mendes.

We followed Lady Azura down the creaky hardwood floor of the hallway, through the purple velvet curtains, and into the séance room.

I stopped in the red foyer, hesitant. Lady Azura was clearly almost as excited about this as Lily. She'd been in already and had lit the candles and drawn the shades. I smelled something cinnamony, with a hint of sweetness.

A resigned sigh escaped me, which I hoped only I heard. I moved into the room and sat down at the round table with Lily and Lady Azura.

Lady Azura reached out and grasped one of each of our hands. Lily and I grasped each other's.

"Lily, is there anyone in particular you would like me to reach? Or shall I just cast a wide net and see who's available?"

Lily's eyes were as wide as saucers. "You can do

that? Just see who wants to come hang out and they'll just join us?"

I started to protest, to tell Lily that was most definitely not how it was done, but Lady Azura silenced me with one of her looks. "Of course I can do that. Close your eyes. Empty your minds."

"You must not set up any barriers, either of you," she continued. I knew she was speaking mostly to me. I tried to empty my mind. Not to block. It wasn't easy. Like being in a dodgeball game and being told not to try to ward off the balls that get thrown at you.

Several long minutes passed. Occasionally Lady Azura would mumble something, but it didn't seem to me like whatever she was doing was working. Lily's hand was warm and dry in my left hand. Lady Azura's felt tiny, papery, but her old fingers still grasped mine firmly.

After a few more moments, Lady Azura cleared her throat and started talking. Her voice sounded even huskier than usual. "I would like to invite our spirit friends that are in our midst to come join us. We are seeking any famous thespians or musicians from the glamorous eras. My lovely young companions wish to delight in the company of the true stars, those of yesteryear. Will anyone oblige us? Marilyn? Elvis? Johnny? Is there anyone there?" This sounded different from what Lady Azura usually said when we were conjuring spirits, but I thought maybe she was putting on a little more of a show for Lily than she did for just me.

I tried to keep my mind open, but this all felt very silly. Stars of yesteryear? Who was going to respond to that?

"Fred?" whispered Lily. "Ginger?"

I opened my eyes. Lily had opened hers as well.

Lady Azura was humming quietly. "I am sensing Irene Dunne. Frederick Arnault. Ella Chase. Please, come through. We would love to have the pleasure of your company if you would care to appear."

I had never heard of those old-time celebrities, but that wasn't all that surprising, as Lady Azura and I were three generations apart, and I didn't watch a lot of old movies.

My eyes were drawn to something in the corner of the room. A silvery glimmer. As quickly as it had appeared, it faded away again. Then, out of the corner of my eye, I thought I saw another shimmery shape, but as soon as I looked at it straight on, there was nothing there. Was I imagining it? I remembered one evening last summer, sitting on the porch with my dad and Lady Azura, watching the fireflies. As soon as one lit up and your eye went to it, it went dark again. I'd had to stare at a dark spot near the hedge and just wait for one to flit by and light up.

I tried this technique now. Looked at a dark corner of the room. Waited for the silvery shimmer. Nothing happened. We were alone. There were no spirits here.

Lady Azura opened her eyes. "Sara," she said in her regular voice, "are you intentionally blocking them?"

"What? No!" My answer came out more forcefully than I had intended.

I took a deep breath and continued. "I don't think there are any spirits here."

Lady Azura dismissed what I had said with a wave of her hand. "They are teetering nearby. I can sense them. But they are not coming through all the way. It is as if they are being blocked." Her eyes met mine.

"Well, if I am blocking them somehow," I said, looking away, "I'm not doing it on purpose."

Lady Azura shrugged and turned to Lily. "I'm sorry,

my dear," she said to her. "But I fear we will not be successful tonight."

Lily looked disappointed, but also a little impressed. "So Sara's powers are so strong that she can cancel yours out?"

"I wouldn't put it that way," Lady Azura said drily. "Though Sara's powers are indeed very strong. But I suspect what is happening here is that Sara is, perhaps unintentionally, preventing the spirits from being able to join us simply because she does not want them to. She's not comfortable with this séance. The vibes in this room are all wrong."

I couldn't tell if Lady Azura was annoyed at me or not. The look on her face was hard to read as she continued talking to Lily. "I believe that I was nearly successful in conjuring these spirits, but they do not feel welcome here"—I started to protest, and she silenced me with a look—"whether that is intentional or not on Sara's part. But they can sense it. As a result, they are stuck. Hesitant to come all the way in. Like a crowded doctor's waiting room. The spirits are lined up and ready to come in, but the doctor isn't seeing patients."

A doctor's waiting room? This made no sense to

me. I wondered if maybe Lady Azura was just making up excuses for not being able to conjure the celebrity spirits Lily had asked for. But a small part of me wondered if I had really blocked them. Could I do that? If I was being really honest, I had to admit that I didn't want them here. Didn't want to do a séance with my best friend and my great-grandmother just for fun. I just wasn't comfortable with it.

I could tell Lily was disappointed, and I felt bad about it. "I'm sorry, Lil," I said. "If I was doing that, I didn't do it on purpose."

Lady Azura clasped my hand. "We believe you, my dear," she said kindly. "Don't we, Lily?"

Lily smiled at me and nodded. "No worries, Sara. I think it's totally cool anyway. Thanks for trying, Lady Azura."

When Lady Azura didn't answer, I looked at her and saw she had walked over to the cabinet where she stored her crystals. "I could also be wrong about the origin of the block," she said distractedly as she carefully peered at some crystals on the shelf. "I sense a tremendous disturbance in the atmosphere."

"What kind of disturbance?" asked Lily.

"It feels weather related," Lady Azura replied as she laid a few crystals out on the table. "It is coming on very quickly, though. I think perhaps a storm is brewing outside."

A storm? Well, that was no big deal. "Well, I guess that makes me feel better, that it's not all my doing," I said.

Lily stood up. "Like I said, no worries," she repeated, playfully tapping me on my shoulder. "I don't know what I would have said to Fred Astaire and Ginger Rogers anyway! Come on. Let's go upstairs and get ready for bed."

We thanked Lady Azura and headed out into the hallway. My dad was coming down the front stairs.

"Oh, good," he said, noticing us right away. "I was coming to look for you. There's a storm coming up the coast that's supposed to make a turn to the west and may head straight for us over the weekend."

"A big one?" asked Lily. "Like one that would cause atmospheric disturbances?"

My dad furrowed his brow and grinned at her good-naturedly. "Could be, Lil," he said. "Right now it's out to sea and categorized as a full-fledged hurricane. Hurricane Seymour, they're calling it. The storm is still quite far south and east of us, and they think it will be downgraded to a tropical storm by Sunday morning," he said. "Still, people in these parts don't play around with big coastal storms. They know how to batten down the hatches. Local businesses are already boarding up, and the lines at the store are getting longer. Our house is close enough to the water that we should take it seriously. Get ready for power outages and that sort of thing."

I swallowed. I'd never been in a hurricane before. Was this what Lady Azura had been sensing? It must be. I was really impressed. But also worried. Weren't hurricanes really serious?

My dad saw my anxious face. He put his arm around me. "Don't worry, kiddo," he said. "Your wonderful father here has already installed the hardware for hurricane panels on all the windows. I'll put up the actual panels tomorrow. We'll be safe and sound if the storm does come."

Lily and I stayed up pretty late talking. She kept saying how lucky I was that I had a great-grandmother as cool as Lady Azura, who could not only talk to spirits, but also know stuff about the weather. It felt good to listen to Lily gush on and on about her. I loved knowing that two of my favorite people liked each other so much.

It was past midnight before we finally unrolled Lily's sleeping bag on the trundle bed. As soon as we were both comfy under our covers, I confessed to her that I had changed my mind about Mason. That I definitely *like*-liked him.

"Well, this is obviously not news to me," said Lily. "I've been able to tell for a while now . . . even if you didn't realize it. Anyway, he likes you too." She was lying on her stomach, the trundle perpendicular to my bed, and had her chin propped in her hands.

"I'm not so sure," I said. "He's so . . . hot and cold with me."

"That's because he's scared of you, Sar," said Lily.

"Why would he be *scared* of me?"

"Have you looked in the mirror? You're totally gorgeous, for one thing."

I flushed and quickly changed the subject. If Mason was scared of me, it was because we shared a freaky secret together. Not because he was intimidated by my looks.

"What about you? I couldn't help but notice you were checking out Calvin yesterday afternoon."

Lily scrambled up to a sitting position. "Oh no! Was it that obvious? Was I acting like a total dork?"

I laughed. "No. I just know you well enough to be able to tell when you're smitten. Kind of like the way you knew I liked Mason before I did."

In the rosy glow of my bedside lamp, I saw a dreamy look appear on Lily's face. "Well, he is pretty amazing-looking, isn't he? And wouldn't it be great if you went out with Mason and I went out with Calvin? We could double-date."

"Yeah," I said. My eyelids were growing heavy. "If only they didn't live two towns away," I said, reaching for the light.

Lily sighed in the darkness. "Yeah. That does stink."

We were sound asleep in minutes.

And then I had another dream.

It was very much like the other one I'd had. In my dream, I found myself standing in the blue bedroom, wearing my nightshirt. The floorboards were cold beneath my feet. Except it didn't feel like nighttime in my dream. It felt like a late afternoon in the winter. Outside I could see that it was snowing. Snow had piled up on the windowsill.

I looked over at the writing desk, knowing what I would see, and I was right. There I sat again, scribbling away in the little book, my long—way longer than real life—hair falling over my face and obscuring my features. But it was me all right.

Even in my dream, it felt weird to address myself. I walked over to me. The other me didn't look up.

"Hey, Sara," I said. "What are we writing about?"

The other me stopped writing. She looked up quickly, and then quickly looked back down. "I'm choosing to ignore you," she said, staring at her book. "Because I know you're not there. You can't be. I'm just imagining you. So please, go away, okay?"

I stood there awkwardly, wondering what to say next. She hadn't started writing again. I could see that her knuckles had grown white, gripping the pen.

Then a shadow moved across the window. I turned toward the opposite wall to see what—or who—was casting the shadow. The weak, late afternoon sun was still bright enough to make it hard to see the dark figure standing in the shadows near the big wardrobe. Was it a man? A woman? A spirit of some sort? All I could see was that it was wearing some odd hat. And then the dream faded and I woke up.

My bedroom was dim but not completely dark. I could see that outside there was an almost-full moon. Lily was breathing regularly next to me. The clock said 4:14. Once again, though, it felt bitter cold. Was the window open a crack?

Moving as quietly as I could, I slid down to the end of my bed and stepped onto the floor. Lily grumbled something, then turned and went back to sleep.

I tiptoed over to the window. It was wide open. Had I forgotten to close it? As I looked outside at the moonlit yard below, I could feel how calm everything was. Not a leaf stirred. There was no wind. All was deathly still. And outside, the air felt weirdly warm. Much warmer than in the room. I closed the window anyway. Tiptoed back to my bed and burrowed under the covers. And the next thing I knew, it was morning.

Chapter 5

"Hey, girls! Get up! It's almost ten!"

I opened my eyes. Sunlight streamed through the windows. Lily was sitting up in bed. I could smell bacon cooking downstairs. And coffee. Even though I'm not a coffee drinker, I still think the smells of bacon and coffee are two of the best smells in the world.

Lily slid off the trundle bed and padded over to the window. She shoved it open, raised the screen, and stuck her nose outside.

"Wow, it's bizarrely warm outside," she said.

The chill I'd felt in the middle of the night was gone. My dream didn't seem quite as eerie by light of day. Now I wished I'd paid more attention to what the other Sara had been writing. And who the spirit was in the room, if in fact it had even *been* a spirit.

"I smell bacon," said Lily. "Do you think it's for us?"

"I'm sure it is. My dad is on a health kick and only eats oatmeal for breakfast these days," I said. "And Lady Azura would never be up this early."

We got dressed quickly and were soon down in the kitchen, where my dad was just pronging the last piece of bacon from the pan and laying it out onto a paper-towel-lined plate.

"Morning, lazy ones," he said, plunking down the plate of bacon and giving my ponytail a playful tug. "Eat up. Change of plans."

Lily was pulling a couple of juice glasses—she knew where everything belonged in our kitchen, just as I did in hers—but she paused and turned toward my dad.

"What's going on?" she asked.

"The storm. It's not being downgraded after all. It's going to remain a hurricane, and it looks like it might be a direct hit on New Jersey tomorrow. They're saying around midafternoon sometime."

Lily and I exchanged looks. My stomach did a little flip-flop.

"So, not to be a party pooper," my dad continued, "but Lily's mom called to say Lily needs to come home to babysit as soon as you two have had breakfast. She and your dad need to get to the grocery store and the hardware store to stock up on supplies in case the power goes out."

"Can I help her?" I asked. Somehow I didn't feel like being by myself to stew about a huge storm if I could help it.

"Sorry, kiddo," said my dad, as he dried a pot from the drainer. "I'll need you around here to help me storm-proof this old place."

I nodded.

After a quick breakfast, we hurried upstairs. I grabbed my camera as Lily packed up her stuff. Then I walked her back to her house. The air was very still, and weirdly warm.

"Do you think this is what they mean by 'the calm before the storm'?" I asked, snapping a picture of the sun peeking through the branches of a tree above our heads.

Lily shrugged. "I don't know. I've never been through a hurricane before. It feels odd around here, though, somehow, in a way I can't really describe."

"It's the light," I said, snapping another picture. "It's a funny yellow-green color. It's really strange."

Lily looked around uneasily. "It's true."

As soon as I got back home, my dad put me to work closing the shutters on all the windows so he could hang the hurricane panels.

"Since the hardware is already installed, I just have to put up the panels and fasten them with wing nuts," he told me, looking pleased with himself.

My dad is king of planning for the worst-case scenario. Now, though, I was very glad to be the daughter of Mr. Disaster Preparedness.

"While you're busy closing the shutters," he said, "I'll be outside sandbagging the casement windows so no water can get in."

I started at the top of the house. My dad had said there wasn't much I could do about the attic windows, which didn't have any shutters for me to close. They were small and round, with thick, old-looking panes of leaded glass that blurred the landscape outside. My dad had told me he would come up later and put up plywood from the inside. But I wanted to be sure my mom's trunk was protected. It was full of her dresses. They were inside an interior room without a window. Lady Azura referred to it as the cedar-lined storage room. After making sure the trunk was sealed tightly and pushed to a far corner, I closed the door to the storage room, feeling satisfied my mom's dresses would be safe.

After closing the shutters in my craft room and the other room on the third floor, I headed to the second floor.

I took care of the shutters in my room, and then my dad's. In the pink room I found one of our resident spirits, seated in her rocking chair as usual, rocking slowly back and forth. I knew her pretty well. When we'd first moved in, I used to hear her crying all the time. But Lady Azura and I had worked with her and helped her cope with her grief for her son, who had died very young. I'm not exactly sure how we did it, but by helping her come to terms with his death, she was somehow reunited with him. She wasn't sad anymore. Sometimes I'd even see her with her spirit baby in her arms.

"Hello," I said cordially. "I hope you don't mind if I just close the shutters. A big storm is coming."

She looked at me, her dark eyes reflecting no light. She nodded and smiled briefly, but then her eyes went back down to the sleeping spirit baby I could now see in her arms. I went about my business quickly and carefully, closing the shutters and making sure they were latched tightly.

"Bye," I said to her as I headed out.

"Please don't be afraid," she said suddenly. "I see in your face that you are concerned about the storm. This house has weathered many, many storms over the years. You should take solace in being home safe and sound, here with your family."

"Thanks," I replied. "You take care in the storm too. You and Angus, I mean." I gestured to the sleeping baby in her arms.

I hesitated on the threshold of the blue bedroom. Though I had been dreaming about it a lot lately, I almost never went in there. It was in this room that I had seen the spirit of the sailor or sea captain or whoever he was. The same one I'd been surprised to see outside of Scoops the other day. He'd never been friendly, or even acknowledged that a modern, living family inhabited this house with him. He was just one of those spirits I'd decided it was best to have nothing to do with. I took a deep breath and hoped he wouldn't be there when I entered.

But when I walked in, there he was.

He stood with his back to me, staring out of the window, the only one in this room that faced the sea. He was muttering something in a low, raspy voice.

I nodded toward him to be polite, even though he didn't seem to know or care that I was there, and moved toward one of the other three windows, so I could get the shutters closed.

I finished closing the first window's shutters and moved to the window in the middle, and closed them. Then, warily, I approached the third window, where he was still standing, muttering.

"Um, excuse me?" I said softly. "I just need to get in here to close the shutters."

". . . the clouds gatherin' thick upon us, and the winds singin' and whistlin' most unusually—"

"Um, see, because there's a storm coming? I'll only be a minute. I just—"

He turned around suddenly, causing me to jump back a little. It was as though he hadn't known I was in the room until this moment. "'Twas the great September gale of '21. We were visited by the winds on a Monday evening, blowin' in from the northeast, swellin' and roarin' as it were by fits. The sky nigh turned black upon us, and my company were not a little shaken."

"Wow, that sounds rough. But, see, I just need to—"

"'Twas a very heavy sea running, and I feared she would part her cables. The stern and bower anchors holding steadily, the wind shifted suddenly four or five points, blowing with increased fury heavily upon the land; the anchors yielding to the force of the winds and waves, began to drag."

"You know what? I'll come back later," I said hastily, edging away from him. Not only was the spirit talking about some storm, but it was really hard to understand his strong accent.

I turned and was about to leave the room when I heard him speak again, this time louder.

"—was like ye as two peas."

That made me stop. Slowly I turned and regarded him.

"*Who* was?" I asked, hardly daring to breathe.

"Tha' art her reflection as she gazes in the looking glass."

Was he talking about my mother? He could have been referring to anyone, really, but something told me, in my gut, that he was talking about my mother. My dad always told me that I looked just like her. Maybe he had seen her, and I was reminding him of her? I knew that she had come to visit Lady Azura in this house, at least a few times, even though I also knew that Lady Azura and my grandmother—Diana, her name was—had not gotten along all that well. But maybe my mother, Natalie, had stayed in this room. I knew she hadn't been able to see spirits, the way I could, but what if this spirit had known *her*? My heart was thudding hard inside my chest.

"Take care. Do not tarry battening the hatches. I'll warrant with the full moon 'twill be as the gale that swept in and tore me sails to pieces. My *Phoebe* lost her bowsprit and was laid upon her beam ends."

I tried to be patient. "Did you—it sounds like you have seen a lot of big storms before. You seem like a knowledgeable sailor. Did you also happen to remember a woman who came to this house from time to time, whose name was Natalie?"

He was starting to shimmer around the edges. "Must hearken to me sloops. The gales are changing direction."

"Please don't go just yet. Did you know someone named Natalie Collins?"

He looked at me with his piercing black eyes, which were the only distinct feature that remained on his rapidly fading self. "Aye, and she left that message for you."

I jumped as though I'd been stung. "A message? What message? My mother left me a message? Where?"

But whether he couldn't or wouldn't answer, the spirit faded away. He was gone.

Chapter 6

I sat down on the bed, releasing a small cloud of dust. I sneezed twice. No one had slept in this room in a very long time, and I doubted anyone had dusted in here either. I stared at the place where the spirit had been.

He was hard to understand, that was for sure. But I was positive he'd said my mother had left me a message. What kind of message?

I needed to talk to Lady Azura.

I finished closing the rest of the shutters on the second floor as fast as I possibly could, which wasn't as fast as I wanted it to be, because some of the old windows were stuck closed by years of paint. But except for one, in the hallway, I got all the shutters closed.

I took the stairs down two at a time and stopped. Would Lady Azura even be awake yet? It was after eleven. Sometimes she didn't emerge until well after twelve.

I met my father in the front hallway.

"I'm heading out for some supplies," he said. "I've got the hurricane panels up on the south and west sides of the house, and I'll finish the rest when I get back."

"Sounds good," I said.

"You okay, kiddo?"

"I guess so. It's just weird to think that there's a storm coming when it's such a beautiful, warm day out."

"Yep. But they're saying it might be a doozy. We have to be prepared for a long power outage and a storm surge. The boardwalk could be in trouble, I'm afraid."

"Have you seen Lady Azura yet today?" I asked.

"She's actually in her séance room," said my dad. "She was up unusually early this morning. She's been scoffing at me for months about my disaster preparedness, but I think now she must be pretty relieved at all the precautions I've taken with this house. I think I heard her in there, stashing breakable stuff away." He grinned. "I tried to explain to her that we live in a different world now. With global warming and the polar ice caps melting, these big storms are unfortunately becoming the new normal."

"Do you think Mom's dresses up in the attic will be safe?" I asked him anxiously.

"Are they closed up in the cedar storage room?" he asked. When I nodded, he smiled at me reassuringly. "They're going to be fine." He gave me a kiss on the top of my head and walked out.

As soon as he'd closed the door, I hurtled through the velvet curtain and into Lady Azura's room, eager to ask her about the sailor spirit.

I was not prepared for what I saw.

Lady Azura was buzzing around her room, arranging crystals and setting out incense, a slightly stricken expression on her face. And milling around *her*, in every square inch of space in that room, were perhaps two dozen spirits. I realized that the dull white noise I was hearing was the sound of a lot of spirits talking all at once.

It seemed our séance the night before *had* worked. All too well.

Lady Azura noticed me almost immediately. "Oh, thank goodness you're here, Sara," she said. "I'm going to need your help. I sense a great deal of atmospheric disturbance both outside and in here."

I raised my eyebrows. I realized she couldn't actually *see* the spirits in here the way I could. But she could sense them. I wondered if she even knew just how many of them were sharing her space at that moment.

"Dahling," said a low voice. A woman spirit drifted toward me. She had to be the spirit of an old-time movie star. I couldn't remember her name; it was someone Lady Azura had loved as a girl, and Lily knew her too. Lily is an old-movie buff.

Her hair was platinum blond, her lips painted dark red, her gown silky and clingy and tightly wrapped around her figure all at the same time. "You requested the pleasure of my company," she continued in her low, throaty voice, "but I must say, I had anticipated something a bit less . . . crowded. I am, after all, accustomed to a private dressing room."

She was obviously a movie star who was used to some pampering, I thought. Before I could respond, another spirit moved toward me.

"Hey, dollface," he said. This one was a man wearing

a pin-striped suit, shiny shoes, and a low-slung hat. I think I remember my dad saying it was called a fedora. He, too, looked like an old movie star, or maybe a private eye or something. "That your grandmother?" he asked, jerking his head toward Lady Azura.

I was a little taken aback by the look on his face. "Um, yes. I mean, no, my *great*-grandmother."

"Well, she looks pretty swell from fifteen feet, and even better from five," he said.

What on earth was he talking about? I think he was paying Lady Azura a compliment, but I wasn't sure. When I glanced over at Lady Azura and saw the pleased smile on her face, I decided it had definitely been a compliment.

I shot her a *What now?* look.

She beckoned me toward her with a small upward gesture of her chin.

I maneuvered through the crowd of spirits and pulled up a chair very close to her.

"The storm must have caused a glitch in the atmospheric pressure and created a delayed response to our summoning the spirits," she said. "In other words, they're coming out of the woodwork. I think they were all lined up last night, waiting to get in from our thwarted séance, and now they're all coming through at once, clamoring for instructions and help for how to get back where they came from."

This information was a relief, actually. I'd been so bothered about the idea that I had blocked Lady Azura's summons without knowing I was doing it. So it hadn't been me after all. It had been the storm. The weird pressure. Still. We had to get rid of these spirits.

"What should we do?" I asked her in a quiet voice. For the moment, I forgot all about the spirit upstairs and his message from my mother.

"I'm trying to clear the air a bit with my crystals and meditation, just to halt some of the confusion before you and I can send everyone on their way," she said.

Lady Azura and I spent the next couple of hours speaking to one spirit after another, politely directing them back to wherever they'd come from and making them think it was their idea, and not ours. I was exhausted by the time we'd gotten rid of the last one—fedora guy, who'd clearly developed a crush on Lady Azura.

As soon as the last spirit had shimmered away and we were left alone, Lady Azura and I sank back into our chairs and exchanged relieved looks.

And then I remembered why I'd come to see her in the first place. I asked her about the sailor spirit I'd seen in the blue bedroom.

"Ah, yes, Duggan," she said.

"Duggan? Do you know his story?"

"I need a cup of tea. Come with me to the kitchen, and I'll tell you what I know of him."

I did, and a few minutes later we were sitting at the kitchen table, me with a bowl of cereal, my second breakfast of the day, and my great-grandmother with her small hands curled around a delicate cup full of steaming tea.

"Duggan lived a very long time ago," my great-grandmother began. "He died in the year 1821. The house he lived in was here, where the present one now stands, but it was torn down not long after he died to make room for a bigger house."

"Was he a sailor?" I asked. "He looks like one."

"He was a shipbuilder," she said. "My dear old friend Harry Jamieson, who died a decade ago, was the town's historian for many years. I learned a great deal from him about the history of Stellamar. It seems there was once a shipyard where the boardwalk now stands, and Duggan was the master builder there."

I set down my spoon. "Is it right where Scoops is located?" I asked.

She nodded.

"That explains why I saw Duggan outside Scoops."

"Ah," she said, nodding her head as if the pieces of a puzzle had just fit together in her mind. "And it would also explain why I have only sensed his presence in the house infrequently. He probably spends whatever time he is here upstairs in the blue bedroom, which has the best view of the ocean. I've noticed over the years that he tends to appear before big storms. Harry told me that Duggan died during a famous hurricane. It made landfall at Cape May in 1821."

"How did he die?"

"I'm not certain, but Harry said there were a great many casualties from the storm. In those days people had little warning before a storm struck. I suppose he must have been swept out to sea while working at his shipyard."

I considered this. I hadn't paid much attention to what Duggan had been muttering, but it did seem to have been about storms. "He seemed to know my mother," I said. "Or at least, I think that's what he said."

"Yes, that's quite possible. Natalie spent some time at the house growing up. A Thanksgiving here, a Christmas there, a week of summer every so often. It's very possible that Duggan remembers her."

"But I think he really *knew* her," I persisted. "At least, I'm pretty sure he told me my mom left me a message. Could she have been able to see him and talk to him when she was alive?"

For a moment, I thought I saw a startled look on Lady Azura's face. But it was gone almost as quickly as it had appeared, and she shook her head. "I'm sorry, Sara, but your mother couldn't see spirits. Our family powers skip some generations. Your mother did not have the gift."

"But anything is possible," I said a little desperately.

"Yes, my dear, anything is possible," she agreed. "But Natalie did not have powers. I would have known. I sensed it in you right away, didn't I?"

She was right about that, but I wanted to believe what Duggan had told me. That my mom had left a message for me.

"Or maybe she sent me the message after she died," I said, more to myself than to Lady Azura, who had gotten up to plug the kettle back in. "Maybe she can't talk to me for some reason and is trying to communicate through him. Duggan."

Lady Azura considered what I had said. She seemed to be speaking even more carefully than usual when she responded. "There is a theory," she said slowly, "that those of us with powers to communicate with spirits in this world have more difficulty communicating with the living after we have passed over."

"*So*," I said eagerly, "if my mother could see spirits, that explains why she hasn't appeared to me. Is that what you mean?"

Lady Azura turned around and leaned against the counter, her eyes closed, as though she was trying to think of a way to let me down gently. "My dear, I am quite sure that Natalie had no powers. There must be some other explanation for what Duggan meant, and we can certainly figure it out. We can ask him the next time we see him."

"But what if—"

"Your phone," Lady Azura said, gently interrupting

me as she pointed to the vicinity of my chair.

My phone was buzzing. I pulled it out of my jeans pocket and checked it. It was a text from Mason.

"Sorry," I said to Lady Azura. "It's a friend of mine who lives closer to the ocean than we do. I've been waiting to hear from him, but it can wait a few minutes."

"Nonsense," Lady Azura said, practically shooing me away from the table as she stood up herself. "I sense this text is important. Go on, and we can discuss this later."

I had the impression that Lady Azura didn't want to talk to me anymore about my mom, which was strange, because she had always been willing to answer all my questions about her in the past. Why was she shutting me down now?

Just then my phone buzzed again as another text from Mason came in. Maybe Lady Azura was right and Mason's texts were really important. I scrolled through the long message.

PARTS OF HARBOR ISLE ARE UNDER A MANDATORY EVACUATION. LOOKS LIKE OUR NEIGHBORHOOD WON'T BE EVACUATED, BUT MY

PARENTS ARE TALKING ABOUT LEAVING ANYWAY. MY MOM IS KIND OF FREAKING OUT. MY DAD IS OUT BUYING SUPPLIES. HOW ARE THINGS IN STELLAMAR? THIS IS TOTALLY INTENSE, RIGHT?

I texted Mason back, and we went back and forth a few times.

YEAH. IT IS DEFINITELY INTENSE. NO EVACUATIONS HERE SO FAR. BUT I AM HATING THIS HURRICANE STUFF.

HEY, LOOK AT THE BRIGHT SIDE. MAYBE THE POWER WILL GO OUT AND WE'LL GET TO STAY HOME FROM SCHOOL.

THAT WOULD BE AWESOME! BUT MAYBE NOT SO AWESOME IF ALL THE LIGHTS GO OUT! WE'D BE LIKE THE PIONEERS, HA HA.

After I hit send, I cringed. Was it dorky to joke about pioneers? And anyway, did it mean anything that Mason had texted me to check in? Was he worried about me? I'd have to tell Lily and see what she thought.

The rest of the day was pretty busy. My dad and I spent the afternoon visiting elderly people on our block and in other parts of the town, helping them seal their windows and check their generators, and going to the store to bring them batteries and flashlights and bottled water. Lily and I had stayed up pretty late the night before, so I was exhausted when I finally climbed into bed that night. Jittery as I felt about the storm, I fell asleep almost immediately.

Chapter 7

I didn't have the dream that night, or if I did, I don't remember it. I slept soundly but woke up earlier than I usually do on a Sunday morning. It was very dark in my room as I glanced at the clock. Only seven thirty. Maybe it was the atmospheric pressure in the air that kept me from rolling over and falling back asleep. For whatever reason, I was wide awake.

I stepped out of bed and groped my way over to my window. Parted the curtains. Remembered that everything was all shuttered up tightly. I couldn't see outside. No wonder it was so dark in here.

Dressing quickly in jeans and an old sweater, I headed downstairs and opened the front door to look outside. The wind had picked up. A lot. Dry leaves danced around in circles across the front walkway. The trees in the yard were whispering and whooshing and swaying back and forth. My hair whipped around my face, in my mouth, my eyes. As I stood there, it began to rain. Fat drops plopped on the front walkway, quickly darkening it until it was shiny and wet. The rain came down harder. Hastily closing the door, I stepped back into the front hall to find my dad emerging from the basement, wiping his hands on a rag stuck into his back pocket.

"Hey, kiddo," he said, giving me a tired smile.

"Hey, Daddy. So what's the latest news on the storm?"

"Things are speeding up. It's due to make landfall by noon," he said. "Come on. Let's go out for breakfast. There's a diner still open in Ocean Heights, and we may as well support our local businesses while we can. And I have a truck full of water, diapers, and long-life milk I promised the church I'd deliver to the shelter over at the high school. Hope my tarp keeps things dry."

So after a quick breakfast, we spent the morning doing more storm preparedness stuff. It kept me so busy I didn't have time to worry about how nervous I was about the storm. I think that might have been my dad's intention all along.

As we drove back toward our house around eleven, there were already lots of small branches down on the road, and it was starting to rain sideways. The windshield wipers were going full speed, and still it was hard to see. My dad pulled the truck into the small garage, and he and I dashed for the house, lugging the last few bags of supplies. We stepped into the kitchen to find Lady Azura calmly reading the paper.

"The pair of you look like you swam here," she said, eyeing us standing on the mat in our dripping raincoats. "Drape your coats over the pantry sink and come have a cup of tea."

My dad and I peeled off our coats. With the windows shuttered, I couldn't see what was happening outside, but I could hear the wind, which rattled the house and seemed to have grown louder in just the past few minutes. I wasn't sure the kitchen, with all its windows, was the best place to be right now.

My dad must have agreed with me. "I think we'd be better off in an interior room," he said. "Why don't we *all* head for the pantry?"

Lady Azura looked like she was about to object, but then we heard a loud bang and the crack of what might have been a large tree limb breaking away, followed by a thud. The lights flickered, but stayed on. Without another word, she picked up her teacup and led the way into the pantry off the kitchen, the two of us following, a tiny queen trailed by her loyal subjects.

It was pretty big, as far as pantries go. Lady Azura had told me before that people used to call it a butler's pantry. There was a small table with three beat-up old stools, and counter-to-ceiling, glass-paneled cabinets. While my dad made a few trips back and forth from the kitchen to the pantry, carrying flashlights and candles and stuff, Lady Azura pulled open a drawer and drew out a deck of cards.

"Are those, like, fortune-teller-type cards?" asked my dad, stopping what he was doing and eyeing the cards warily.

Lady Azura smiled. "No, Mike, dear. They're just cards. I thought we could—"

There was a crash of thunder and then the lights went out, plunging us into darkness.

I gave a little surprised squeak. But a second later my dad had turned on a flashlight, and then a camping lantern lit the small room up with a warm glow.

"I'll shuffle," said my dad with a wry grin.

The three of us sat down to play. We played Hearts, and gin rummy, and even Go Fish—which had been my favorite game when I was a little kid. We played for what felt like hours, but I wasn't bored for a second. Despite all the madness that was going on outside, I felt warm and safe and happy. At one point my dad ventured out into the kitchen with a flashlight and, promising to be super alert and careful near the windows, made us some grilled cheese sandwiches on the gas-powered stove.

While my dad was preparing our lunch, Lady Azura and I talked more about Duggan.

"Have you seen him your whole life?" I asked her.

"I used to see him often when I was younger. He frequented the blue room on the second floor if I recall correctly." She smiled wryly. "But as I haven't been upstairs in years, I haven't seen much of him."

I nodded. Waited. You couldn't rush Lady Azura into giving you essential information. You had to let her tell you on her own terms.

"I used to see him just before a big storm. He seemed to appear just as the weather was about to turn, and then he'd disappear again. Perhaps to where his old shipyard used to be. I never really put it together before now, but he seems to be drawn out by the weather. It makes sense, given the circumstances of his death."

"Well, that was where I saw him on Thursday. Where his shipyard used to be. Just outside Scoops. But he doesn't seem to know or care if I can see him."

"Yes, he was always rather gruff," said Lady Azura primly. "But he was from another era."

Because Lady Azura seemed to be more comfortable talking about Duggan now, I decided to bring my mom up again. I took a deep breath and plunged right in. "I'm positive he told me that my mom had left a message for me. I know it sounds crazy, but I got the impression that he has something more to tell me about her. Can I go see if he's upstairs?"

Lady Azura pursed her lips. "Best wait until after the storm," she said.

And then my dad came back with a platter of grilled cheese sandwiches, which ended the conversation about Duggan.

But I couldn't stop thinking about him. I had to go

find him, talk to him. See what he had meant about the message.

We ate our lunch, and then my dad made tea for Lady Azura, and it wasn't long after she'd finished her first cup that we became aware that the winds seemed to have died down, and that the rain wasn't pounding down with so much force anymore. The storm seemed to have passed.

We all headed into the kitchen, and my dad opened the door. Lady Azura and I followed him out onto the stoop.

The rain had stopped. The winds were still blowing but nowhere near as hard. Dark, puffy clouds zoomed across the sky like they'd been filmed with a time-lapse camera. Branches and leaves were all over the place.

"I'm going to check the exterior for damage," said my dad.

"I'll check the interior," I said quickly, knowing this was my chance to seize the opportunity to look for Duggan upstairs.

Lady Azura gave me a look. She knew what I was up to, of course.

"I, for one, shall go have my nap," she said in her queenlike voice. "This has been quite enough excitement for me for one day."

My dad gave her a flashlight to light her way through the still-dim kitchen. Then he headed outside to go inspect for any damage.

I searched the house from top to bottom. I saw the spirit of the woman in the pink bedroom, and I saw grumpy Mr. Broadhurst walking back and forth in our sitting room on the second floor. I even saw Henry in the closet of my crafts room. He had a lot of questions about the storm and why it had been so dark and loud. I explained as best I could.

I did not see Duggan.

Chapter 8

We got our power back the next morning, Monday, but on the news I learned that school would be closed through Wednesday. Lily got her power back around the same time as we did, but she told me that parts of Stellamar might be out for a while—particularly the parts nearest to the shore. I didn't hear anything from Mason. I assumed his power was out and that he wasn't able to text me because of the spotty cell phone service. I hoped he was okay. And that his house was okay. For all I knew, his family had ended up getting evacuated after all.

My dad let me head over to Lily's house on Monday afternoon, after he'd made sure there were no dangerous power lines down or anything. That's how I learned about Mason's school.

Lily was related to every other person in Stellamar,

or at least it seemed like it sometimes. She had a lot of relatives in the volunteer fire department and the local police departments, so as usual, I learned more from her than from the TV.

"Harbor Isle Middle School had a *lot* of damage," Lily told me. "A tree fell on the cafeteria roof! And a bunch of the ground-floor classrooms got flooded after the windows broke. So the school has to close, maybe for months, while they repair it."

My eyes widened.

"I know, right? They're going to move a bunch of the kids into the high school, but at least a hundred are going to have to get bused to schools in neighboring towns, at least through January. Including Stellamar."

Mason. Would Mason be allowed to come to our school?

Lily read my mind. Not really. But kind of.

"I know what you're thinking, but you can stop thinking it," she said. "My mom talked to Mason's mom, and he's going to Ocean Heights. Which makes his parents mad because Mason's closest friends are getting sent here."

Oh well.

"What about Calvin?" I asked. "Is he one of those friends?"

Lily shook her head, an exasperated expression on her face. "I don't know. I haven't been able to find out. I couldn't exactly ask my mom to ask Mason's mom, because what if word got back to Calvin? He'd know it was me asking. I'm definitely keeping my fingers crossed. But I don't even know his last name."

I kept pretty busy the next few days. My dad and I made big pots of spaghetti and delivered meals to several of our elderly neighbors who were without power.

And I searched for Duggan, keeping my eyes peeled as my dad and I drove around town, looking for Duggan's distinctive sailor hat. But he was nowhere to be found. The blue bedroom remained spirit free. On Tuesday I grabbed my camera and walked to Scoops in the hopes I might find him around there. The boardwalk was eerily quiet, with most of the shops still boarded up. I noticed that in one place the railing of the boardwalk had been completely torn away by the winds. My dad had told me that we had been really lucky, that the dunes on the beach had really held up and helped to protect the boardwalk and the neighborhoods closer to the shore in Stellamar, but I knew some other towns hadn't been so lucky. Towns like Harbor Isle. I didn't find Duggan, but I did get some pretty incredible pictures of the aftermath of the storm.

On Tuesday night I finally heard from Mason. He told me his house was still out of power but otherwise had done okay. A big tree had come down but luckily hadn't hit his house. But parts of his town were in really bad shape. He and his parents were staying with his grandparents for a few days until the power came back on at home, or until they figured something else out.

My dad stayed home Monday and Tuesday, as his office had lost power, but he kept busy helping neighbors with repairs and stuff. Several times I thought of telling my dad about Duggan. But in the end, I didn't. He knew about my powers, of course. But he still seemed uncomfortable talking openly about spirit stuff. And since this spirit stuff had to do with my mom, I was afraid of completely freaking him out.

On Wednesday, Lady Azura found me staring out of the bay window toward the ocean.

"Brooding over this message business with Duggan?" she asked me.

I whirled around, feeling upset and thinking she didn't believe me or take me seriously. But when I saw her face, I saw a look of genuine concern. And a lot of love.

I shook my head. "I've searched the house twice," I said, "even though I have no idea what I'm looking for. And I don't know if he said he has a message my mother left me while she was alive, or if she sent me a message more recently, and even though I've looked and looked, I—"

"Perhaps we can conjure him."

"—like, up in the attic," I continued, because her words hadn't registered. "And even—" Her words sank in. I gaped at her. "Wait. *What* did you say?"

"I said perhaps we can conjure him."

"Duggan? Really? Can we?"

She nodded. "I don't see why not. We've certainly been all too successful summoning other spirits recently. There's no reason we can't try to summon him."

"Can we do it now?" I asked eagerly.

She nodded. "Come. Follow me to my fortune-telling room."

I practically ran into her room after her. Helped her light candles. Pulled the shades. Arranged crystals. As fast as I could. And then we sat down across from each other, and I tried to clear my mind. To stop it from blocking anything out.

We held hands across the table and closed our eyes.

"Mr. Duggan," said Lady Azura in her low, velvety voice, the one I had grown accustomed to hearing by now in her séance room. "Mr. Duggan. We invite you to visit us."

We waited. Waited some more. I opened one eye. I sensed nothing. It wasn't going to work. I felt the despair take hold of me.

And then I sensed something.

I opened my eyes slowly. Looked around the room, into the dark, shadowy corners.

There.

A figure stood, a dark-gray silhouette against the pale daylight that was glowing faintly behind the drapery. The figure moved. Stepped out of the shadows and into the candlelit circle of our table.

It was Duggan.

But a very young Duggan.

He wore the same blue coat, but it was new-looking and unsoiled, not yet threadbare near the shoulders and elbows. His face was clean-shaven, his jet-black hair just barely caught up in a small ponytail at the nape of his neck. On his head he wore a brown, three-pointed hat. Possibly the same one worn by his old self, but this one was new-looking, without scuffs or shiny spots where the suede had worn away.

I stood up from my chair, so excited to see him that I let it crash backward to the floor. Lady Azura winced at the noise, but it didn't seem to bother Duggan the spirit.

"Thank you," I said in a high-pitched voice. "For coming. Here, I mean. To see us."

He grunted, his heavy dark eyebrows turned downward.

"So, Mr. Duggan," I said, trying not to sound nervous. "Okay if I ask you a question?"

Lady Azura was allowing me to speak, to direct this conversation. I was grateful for that.

He nodded. "Aye."

"I'm wondering. My name is Sara. My mother is—was—Natalie. I was just wondering if you knew her."

His dark eyes bored into mine. I waited, my breath caught in my throat, hardly daring to breathe.

"Nay, I duh'nt know 'er," he said at last.

My heart sank. "But—but I thought you had a message. From her. For me," I said weakly. I willed myself to swallow the huge lump that had risen in my throat. Not to cry. Not now.

He shook his head, and for the first time I noticed a heavy gold earring in one of his ears. "Nah, I duh'nt know 'er," he repeated. He looked from me to Lady Azura. "Must return to me ship, the *Phoebe*. She's at the docks. Beautiful, she is."

Before I could think of anything else to say, he shimmered away and vanished.

I stared at Lady Azura. "Did you see him?"

She shook her head. "I could not see him. But I sensed his presence, and I could hear him quite well."

"Well, what do you think is wrong? Was he lying to me? Or had he been lying before, about having a message from my mother?" Hot tears sprang to the corners of my eyes.

Lady Azura patted the table gently, indicating that I should sit back down. I sat.

"I believe he was telling the truth both times," she said quietly.

That made no sense. I started to say something.

"I believe that this Duggan is a younger version of the spirit you met upstairs. Did he *look* younger?"

I reflected. "Well, yes. Definitely. But—"

"I believe he truly doesn't know who Natalie is—yet."

I didn't understand. She could see by my face that I didn't.

"Some spirits who stay tied to the earth after they die go through cycles. They will relive various parts of their former lives. I believe that Duggan as a spirit does what the living Duggan did many years ago. He spends part of his time here, in the house, and part at the shipyard, and part at sea. We happened to conjure the younger man."

"That's crazy," I said. "Why would he do that?"

"Do you remember that my late husband Richard appears to me on Christmas?"

"Yes," I said.

"Sometimes he appears as a young man, and sometimes he appears as he did later in his life. There are no hard-and-fast rules with spirits. They really get to do whatever they want."

"Maybe we can try again. Maybe if we try to invite the old Duggan this time—"

She shook her head. "I'm afraid it doesn't work that way."

"But how do you know?" I pressed. "I mean, can't we try at least?"

"Sara, please believe me that I know what I am talking about here. I have a lot of experience with this. As I said, my late husband, Richard, comes to me in various forms. Believe me when I tell you I have tried to send back the very young Richard when he appears, and trade him in, so to speak, for my favorite Richard, in his midfifties. But I cannot do so. And in the process I have managed to really confuse the spirit who is with me."

I believed her, of course. And I could imagine that it would be pretty confusing for a spirit, who maybe didn't even grasp that he was a spirit in the first place, to be asked to leave and come back as himself thirty years later. I swallowed my bitter disappointment and decided to head over to Lily's.

I told her everything, of course.

We were up in her room, packing boxes full of shoes that Lily and her mother had collected from the basement for a clothing drive. Buddy, the Randazzo family dog, lay sprawled on the floor among all the shoes, sound asleep and snoring contentedly. Lily sat on the floor next to him, one hand on his head, the other holding a pink sneaker in her hand. She looked at it thoughtfully. "I have an idea," she said.

I looked up from my box and sat back on my heels. From the tone of her voice, it sounded like it might be a big idea. I waited expectantly.

"Why don't you and I try to conjure him with my spirit board?" she suggested.

I grimaced. "I don't know. The last two times I've tried to conjure spirits have been pretty disastrous." I realized that in all the excitement of the storm, I hadn't yet told her about the crowd of spirits that had shown up after the session we'd had together with Lady Azura. So I filled her in on what had happened.

Lily wouldn't be dissuaded. "Well, this time it

wouldn't be just for the fun of it. We'd be very specifically calling to one spirit. Anyway, it's an idea. Think it over."

I promised I would.

We spent the rest of our time home from school keeping busy with post-storm cleanup. I helped Lily's parents get their yard back in shape. There was a lot of un-prepping to do around Lily's house: We picked up all the sticks and branches that had blown down in the yard and packed up more boxes for the clothing drive. Lily and my dad and I also helped our neighbors pick up sticks and stuff in their yards. And I took more pictures.

I was actually happy when school resumed on Thursday morning.

Chapter 9

Thursday morning Principal Bowman called an all-school assembly to introduce the new kids from Harbor Isle. All twenty of them stood on the stage in a clump, and Mrs. Bowman introduced them one by one.

Mason was not among them.

"I don't see Calvin," whispered Lily, who was sitting beside me. "I guess he's not going to be here."

"Sorry, Lil," I said.

Jody Jenner was there, though. The girl I'd met the week before at Scoops. There was a smattering of applause as Mrs. Bowman called out Jody's name, and she waved to the crowd like she was the president, a big smile on her pretty face.

Beside me, I could hear Lily grumbling under her breath.

"What's up?" I whispered to her.

"Nothing," she whispered back. "I just don't trust her. Something tells me she's not as nice as everyone thinks she is."

I shrugged. "Well, you've known her longer than I have. I'll—"

"Calvin Kennedy," called Mrs. Bowman.

I felt Lily start. I grinned. Gave her a little elbow in the arm.

Calvin emerged from where he'd been standing in the back of the clump. I had to admit, he really was nice-looking. I could understand Lily's obsession. In a purely objective way, of course.

Mrs. Bowman called the last few kids' names and then explained that the Harbor Isle kids would be with us for the rest of the semester—most likely until the new year. And that we should welcome them, show them around, help them find their way to classes. I made a promise in my head to be as welcoming as I could.

I knew what it was like to be new. It wasn't that long ago that I was the new girl at Stellamar Middle School. I just couldn't help but feel let down that Mason wasn't one of the new kids.

I gave Lily another nudge with my elbow. She nudged back.

Well, at least Lily could focus on *her* crush.

At lunch, Miranda waved over Jody and her friend, Caroline, inviting them to come sit at our table. We all moved over to make room for them.

Caroline sat across the table, between Tamara and Marlee. Jody sat down between me and Lily. "I see the food here is as delicious as it is at Harbor Isle," she said drily, poking at her lukewarm slice of pizza.

"Yeah, the kitchen got a four-star rating in the *New York Times* recently," I said.

Jody laughed.

Was Lily right about her? I wondered. She seemed really nice.

"So is your dad really a famous TV director guy?" asked Avery eagerly.

Jody rolled her eyes. "I guess you would say so," she said, taking a dainty sip of her chocolate milk. "But to me he's just a random dad, as embarrassing as the next dad."

We all laughed at that. She seemed so normal.

"Hey, tell them about how you stayed in that

castle this summer, and your ghost story," suggested Caroline.

"You stayed in a castle?" asked Miranda, her eyes round.

"With a *ghost*?" added Tamara.

I swallowed hard.

"Yeah," said Jody. "We were visiting this guy who was in one of my dad's TV movies. John Fry."

"Wait. You mean, *John Fry*, John Fry? The guy who stars in that new TV show?" asked Miranda.

"Oh. Yeah, I guess he has a show, too."

We all knew the show, of course. It was a huge hit, a drama about a guy who has secret superpowers for fighting bad guys. John Fry was this twentysomething, super-gorgeous British movie star who was on the cover of every weekly magazine at the grocery check-out counter.

"Anyway," Jody continued, "so John owns this huge, rambling castle in Scotland, with a moat and servants and everything, and supposedly there's a ghost that haunts it, the ghost of a young girl who threw herself off a parapet a few centuries ago."

"Why?" asked Tamara, transfixed.

"I guess because she couldn't marry the guy she loved. Something like that."

"And you *saw* her? The ghost, I mean?" asked Marlee.

"Well, maybe yes, maybe no," said Jody. "I mean, I woke up in the middle of the night and was sure I saw a girl in a long white dress standing in my room. Then she vanished. And the next morning when I asked about it, John's wife told me that was the very room where the girl had once slept."

This story seemed to impress everyone at the table. I wasn't sure what to say, so I kept quiet. Of course.

Unfortunately, Avery didn't.

"Well, *Sara* here has a great-grandmother who can see spirits," she said. "And she's totally famous. Just last spring she helped catch a burglar. She was in the news and everything."

Jody looked at me, and I saw a flicker of disapproval pass across her face. A second later, though, she was smiling again. Had I imagined it?

"Collins!" a voice boomed at me from across the cafeteria. I jerked my head up to look, although I realized who it was before I even saw him.

SARANORMAL

It was the spirit of a gym teacher, long since dead. He bothered me regularly at school, starting back on my very first day last year. I generally managed to avoid him. But today he seemed intent on talking to me. I realized with dread that he was striding through the crowded cafeteria, right in my direction.

I stood up quickly. "Got to go print something out in the library," I mumbled, collecting my tray and my backpack and disentangling myself from the table. I noted the perplexed looks on the faces of some of my friends at the table, but better to let them think I was being weird and impulsive than having them see me in a close encounter with a loudmouthed spirit.

I made it to the side of the cafeteria, with a clear passage to the doorway, but he stepped in front of me, his barrel chest heaving, and stuck a chubby finger in my face.

"I got a job for you, Collins," he said.

"Not now," I said out of the side of my mouth, hoping no one was looking my way. I tried to move past him, but he blocked my way again.

"I need to give you something to bring to someone," he said.

I knew what I had to do. I had to be firm with him.

"Listen," I said, still out of the corner of my mouth, and trying to edge my way out with my back to the wall. "You can't approach me like this in front of—"

"Who exactly are you talking to?" said a voice over my shoulder.

I froze. Turned. It was Jody.

"Oh. I—ah-ha-ha!" I stammered. My mind had gone blank. But at least the spirit had vanished.

"We're supposed to memorize a passage from *Julius Caesar*," I heard Lily say. She was there, just behind Jody. "You were just practicing your lines, right, Sar?"

I shot her a grateful look. "Yep. I was just memorizing a passage from *Julius Caesar*. Guess I shouldn't talk out loud like that, huh," I said.

"Yeah, maybe not," Jody replied. But then she smiled. "Hey, Sara," she said in a really friendly voice. "It's Sara, right?"

I nodded.

"Listen, I was just telling the rest of the table something when you jumped up and left. We're organizing a fund-raiser. For the storm victims. It's going to be a joint event between Stellamar Middle and Harbor

Isle Middle. An auction. The PTA asked my parents
to help with it, since my dad knows a bunch of celebrities and stuff. They want him to auction off a visit
to his TV studio, maybe even a bit part in one of his
upcoming episodes." She said it really casually, like it
was no big deal. "Anyway, do you want to come over
to my house with a bunch of kids tomorrow night to
help plan it?"

"Oh! Sure! That sounds great," I said.

Lily winked at me. "Lots of kids are going to be
there, probably even some kids who didn't get transferred to Stellamar. . . ."

Jody frowned when Lily said that. But only for a
moment.

"When is the auction going to be?" I asked.

The bell rang, and suddenly there was noise and
confusion as kids started moving toward the door for
their next class.

"Gotta go! See you in English!" Lily said, and then
she hustled off.

"To answer your question," said Jody, "it's going to
be a week from tomorrow."

I stopped. "Oh no. That's the night I have to go

with my dad to a wedding. I promised him I'd be his date."

"Oh, that's too bad," said Jody quickly. "Well, then I guess there'd be no reason for you to come tomorrow night for the planning, if you can't be there for the auction. You'd just feel left out. Don't even worry about coming. Sorry!" she said, drawing out the word dramatically. "See you later!"

And she turned on her heel and hurried away, leaving me standing there with my mouth open.

Had she just gone from really friendly to really weird in about two seconds flat? And uninvited me to a really fun get-together tomorrow night? It seemed that she had.

Chapter 10

I spent a glum Thursday evening at home that night, doing homework, thinking about the get-together I had been uninvited to that would be happening the next night, and dwelling on the unfair fact that Mason hadn't been one of the Harbor Isle kids transferred to my school. I thought about texting Lily to tell her what had happened with Jody moments after she'd walked away. But I didn't. Lily would probably not go either, out of loyalty to me. And I wanted her to go. Because Calvin would be there. It was a perfect opportunity for her to see him in a relaxed setting. And also, I didn't want to do anything to make things worse between Lily and Jody. I was beginning to think that maybe Lily's gut feeling about Jody was right—that she wasn't very nice after all—though I was really trying to keep an open mind.

But contributing most to my glum mood was the fact that Duggan had not returned. I'd sat in the blue bedroom reading for almost two hours, hoping he would show up, but he didn't. I was beginning to believe that he might never return. That I'd never get the message my mother had sent me.

I was also confused about Mason. Why hadn't he texted me in the past few days? Why was he the only one in his whole friend group that wasn't attending Stellamar? Was he avoiding me?

And then the next day, Friday, as I was approaching my locker in the morning hallway traffic, I practically ran into him. Mason.

He was there. At Stellamar. Looking very student-like, with his backpack slung over one shoulder and his headphones clamped around his neck.

I'm not sure which of us was more surprised to see the other one. We both stood there, staring at each other.

Mason spoke first.

"Hey," he said.

"Hey," I said. I waited for him to explain.

"Guess you're surprised to see me, huh?"

"Um, yeah. I thought you got shipped out some-where else. Calvin told us Ocean Heights Middle School."

He nodded. "Yeah, that was the plan at first. But my mom pulled some strings. When we learned that Cal and a couple of my other friends were all coming here, she called the principal and asked her if I could be sent here. It took an extra day, but they made it happen." He grinned a little sheepishly. "So here I am."

I could feel a dumb grin spreading across my face. I tried not to act too psyched. But I was.

"Mason? No way!" shrieked a voice behind me.

I turned and saw Jody.

Jody gave Mason a big hug. This alarmed me. The jealousy roiled around inside me, even though I told myself they were just friends. That she had a boyfriend in high school. But still. A gorgeous girl was hugging my crush.

"So you made it to Stellamar!" she squealed, clasp-ing her hands and bouncing a little. "That is awe-*some*."

"Yeah, well, I was just, ah, talking about it with Sara here," said Mason.

I appreciated that he was trying to include me in

the conversation. Jody kind of half nodded in my direction and then turned her attention back to Mason.

"Hey, listen, Mace," she said.

Mace?

"I'm having a get-together at my house tonight to plan for the auction next week. Can you come over? Like, around seven? We're ordering tons of takeout and stuff."

Mason glanced at me, and then at Jody. "Sure," he said. "Sounds cool."

The bell rang. We all had to get to class.

So Mason was definitely going to be at the get-together tonight. And I definitely was not going to be.

I was thinking the day couldn't get worse. And then it did.

I was heading out of social studies class when I almost ran smack-dab into the gym teacher spirit.

"Collins!" he said.

I groaned inwardly.

"I'll walk with you," he said, noticing that everyone was moving toward their next class. Without waiting for me to agree, he hitched up his polyester-looking gym pants and fell into step alongside me. Out of the corner of my eye I noticed he was in a semitransparent state, and that as we walked side by side, real kids heading in the other direction passed right through him without feeling his presence.

I pulled out my copy of *Julius Caesar* and opened it to a random page so it would look as though I was reading words out loud to myself. Maybe people would think I was trying to recite lines from memory, rather than talking to some invisible person next to me. I hoped so. "Listen," I said in a low voice, still staring down at the book. "It's not that I'm trying to be rude. It's just that I'm in school. I need you to leave me—"

". . . a message. For you."

I stopped and stared at him. We'd been talking over each other, without listening to what the other was saying. But suddenly I was all ears.

"Did you just say something about a message?" I asked him. I noticed some passing sixth graders had turned around to look at me curiously. I stared back down at *Julius Caesar*.

"Did you just say something about delivering a message?" I asked again, still looking down at my book. Did he mean the message Duggan had spoken about?

Had he found it somehow? Did he know Duggan?

"Yep. I need you to go see Evelyn Diamond. She lives at the Cherry Hill Retirement Home," he said, his voice getting lower and gruffer than usual. "Tell her from me that Barkus was—" He took a breath. Swallowed. Dabbed at a corner of his eye. Cleared his throat and began again. "Tell her Barkus luh-loved her. That he was on his way to ask her to marry him when—when a truck passed him going the other direction, and it had crossed over the middle line, and that Barkus swerved his pickup and slid off the road and, well, he—that is, I—never got the chance to tell her." He sniffed loudly. "I was a darn fool to have waited so long."

I nodded. His message had nothing to do with me. It was just some unfinished business he had, that he needed my help taking care of. I had learned from Lady Azura that sometimes spirits are trapped here, in our world, because they have stuff they need to take care of. I was obligated to do my best to help him. I looked up and saw tears shimmering in his eyes. I felt a lump in my own throat and swallowed it back. We'd arrived at my classroom. The second bell was about to ring.

I stared down at my book and spoke to him. "Mrs. Diamond?" I asked.

"Miss. *Miss* Diamond. She never married. I was too lunkheaded to get up the nerve to ask her until it was too late," he said. "She taught home ec. She used to bring me baked goods her students had made." He produced a large handkerchief from somewhere and blew his nose so loudly I couldn't believe the whole school couldn't hear it. But no one heard him except me.

The bell rang. I turned to him. "Okay. I'll go this afternoon," I said. "I promise."

"Good show, Collins," he said. "Tell her I was a lunkhead, remember." He was beginning to fade. "I knew you were varsity material the day I first laid eyes on you!"

He faded away to nothing. I smiled and hurried into my classroom.

Chapter 11

Cherry Hill Retirement Home looked more like a condominium complex than a nursing home. When I pushed open the wide, handicap-accessible doors, I braced myself for the worst. I hate nursing homes. Back in California, I'd once had to go with my dad to visit his great-uncle, and the place smelled awful, of medicine and disinfectant masking some other, darker odors. When we got to his room, my dad's great-uncle didn't even recognize him.

But Cherry Hill was not a bit like that awful place. It was cheerful. Sun streamed in, and there were potted plants in the hallways. The windows were hung with checkered curtains that looked like someone had spent a lot of time sewing them.

The lady at the front desk cheerfully directed me toward the sitting room, telling me I'd find Miss

Diamond watching her favorite show on the Home and Garden channel.

There were several old people sitting around the sitting room, but just one who seemed to be interested in what was on TV—it was a craft show teaching people how to make hats out of margarine tubs.

Miss Diamond was tiny, maybe even smaller than Lady Azura. She was wrapped in a hand-crocheted pink shawl and wearing a teal-blue, pleated skirt. I wondered if she'd sewn it herself.

"Excuse me, Miss Diamond?" I whispered.

She didn't turn from her show.

I tried again, louder. "Miss Diamond?" I repeated.

She turned, and then tilted up her chin and peered at me. Her eyes behind her glasses were enormous. She tilted her chin back down. "Sit down, young lady," she commanded.

I sat. She still had her teacher's way about her.

"Your name, child?"

"Sara Collins, ma'am."

"You're a pretty thing. Lovely hair and eyes. Do you know how to knit?"

"Knit?" I asked, startled. "Um, no."

She shook her head. "Kids these days. What do they teach them in those schools?" She turned to me. "Don't tell me. You're here to do a report about the Great Depression for school and you need to interview someone."

"Um, not exactly."

"Well I wasn't alive during the Civil War, so don't ask me about that."

"No, ma'am. I'm here to—to, well, I know it sounds strange, but I'm here to give you a message."

"A message."

"Yes. From—from Mr. Barkus."

She jerked her chin up and stared at me for a long time, like a fish in an aquarium. Searched my face. I guess she decided I wasn't making fun of her or playing some awful joke, because slowly she lowered her chin and leaned in toward me.

"Mr. Barkus has given you a message for me?" Her voice was suddenly soft.

"Yes, ma'am. You see, I—well, I can see him. And talk to him."

She nodded. Like I'd just said something totally ordinary.

"Perhaps you think me an old fool for believing you," she said.

"No, ma'am. I'm actually really relieved that you do."

"Humph. Well, the older I get, the more willing I am to believe such things," she said. "All right, child. Tell me. What is the message Mr. Barkus asked you to deliver to me?"

"He asked me to tell you that he—he loved you. That he was on his way to ask you to marry him the night that his pickup slid off the road. That he should have told you earlier, but he was a . . . a big lunkhead."

I sat with my hands folded in my lap and waited for her to say something.

She was quiet for a very long time. Then a slow smile spread across her wrinkly face. A glint of a tear appeared in the corner of her eye.

"That old fool," she said, shaking her head and continuing to smile. "I know you're telling me the truth, because he used that word a lot. Lunkhead."

She reached out and patted my hand, and then turned away, pulling an embroidered white hanky out from the folds of her shawl. "Thank you, pretty young girl," she said, over her shoulder. "You've made an old lady very happy."

When I left a little while later, I had a big smile on my face.

That evening I had dinner with Lady Azura. My dad was working late. I made us omelets and toast. I was glad that my visit with Miss Diamond had been so pleasant. I was almost able to not dwell on the fact that all my friends were currently at Jody Jenner's house, having a fabulous time. Without me.

"You came home late this afternoon," Lady Azura remarked, taking a dainty bite of her omelet.

"I had to run an errand. At Cherry Hill Retirement Home," I said.

She waited. Picked up her teacup and took a sip, her large, honey-brown eyes regarding me above the rim as she did so.

I realized I needed to explain. I told her about my errand on Mr. Barkus's behalf.

Lady Azura was beaming by the time I finished my story.

"I knew the both of them," she said.

I looked at her in astonishment.

"Miss Diamond taught us home ec," she said. "She was a lovely young woman, and it was her first year of teaching. She didn't look much older than we were, although I suppose she had to be. In those days, girls took home ec and boys took shop. I never knew she and Mr. Barkus were closely acquainted. He was a coach, and I had very little interaction with him. Because girls didn't do sports in those days either."

I reflected on this. It was kind of hard to believe how much she had lived through during her lifetime. All those changes she'd witnessed.

"But I do remember hearing of his death years after I graduated." She shook her head. "You did a lovely thing today. I am sure Mr. Barkus won't be hounding you quite so much at school anymore. And that lovely Miss Diamond." She sighed. "You're never too old to experience true love."

I sighed. "Well, I know what it feels like not to be able to receive a message. If I can't get Duggan to deliver a message from my mother, at least I can make sure others receive *their* messages."

She patted my hand. "Good things come to those

who wait, my dear," she said. "If there is a message waiting for you from your mother, it will reveal itself when the time is right."

I wanted to believe her. Wanted to think that I would find out what the message was. But I was getting impatient. I didn't like waiting. I'd been waiting for thirteen years already. How much longer did I have to wait?

We heard my dad's tires crunching on the gravelly driveway. A moment later he was coming through the kitchen door. I jumped up to set a place for him, and began cracking eggs into a bowl.

My dad sat down wearily at the kitchen table and loosened his tie while I dropped a pat of butter into the pan. As it sizzled, I plugged the teakettle back in.

"Listen, kiddo," he said to me. "I saw Lily's mom today when I was leaving for work. She told me about the auction that's happening next Friday. And how it's the same night as Costi's wedding. The auction sounds like a big deal. Would you rather go to that and not come to the wedding? I'd understand if you wanted to do that."

I poured my dad a cup of tea, then dumped the eggs into the pan and swirled them around as it sizzled, smelling delightfully of butter. "Dad, I'm going to the wedding with you," I said firmly, plunking the tea down in front of him.

He and Lady Azura exchanged glances.

"I've spent a lot of time with the spirit in the pink bedroom," I explained. "So I understand what it means to appreciate your family. I'm going to the wedding."

My dad knew who I was talking about. I had told him a little bit about her, and how her baby had died and she used to cry all the time.

"That's a lovely way to look at the world, Sara," said Lady Azura approvingly.

My dad smiled at me. Then he curled his large hands around his mug of tea and stared off into space.

I knew that look. He was remembering my mother.

The next morning, Saturday, I awoke to feel a heavy weight on my legs. I couldn't move them. It was as though they'd turned to concrete.

I opened my eyes.

Lily was sitting on me.

"Wake up, lazybones!" she said, and bounced up and down a few times for emphasis.

"Ow!" I said.

She stood up a little, releasing my pinned legs and allowing me to sit up in bed, rubbing my eyes against the sunlight. She must have opened the shades upon entering my room.

"What time is it?" I mumbled blearily, looking at the clock.

"It's practically nine a.m.!" she said.

"It's eight thirty-nine," I countered. With a groan, I fell back down against my warm pillows.

"I came to tell you about the meeting last night," said Lily. "Why didn't you tell me you weren't going to be there? I would never have gone if I'd known you weren't going!"

For a moment I thought about not telling Lily what had happened between me and Jody. But who was I kidding? Of *course* I was going to tell my best friend.

"I thought I was going," I said. "But then I got uninvited. By Jody. And I knew if I told you that, you wouldn't go, and I *wanted* you to go so you would be able to hang out with Calvin."

Lily's eyes narrowed.

I told her what had happened, about the

conversation I'd had with Jody in the cafeteria on Thursday, after Lily had left us.

"Well, no wonder," she said, crossing her arms and glowering. "Mason was asking me why you weren't there, and I had no idea. But Jody definitely heard him asking me. And she chose not to say anything. I tell you, Sar, I don't trust that girl."

I sat back up and hugged my knees to my chest underneath my warm covers. "I think she means well," I said uncertainly. "She said she didn't want me to feel left out, because I wasn't going to be at the fund-raiser next week."

Lily looked at me skeptically. I decided to try and change the subject. "Well, so, how was it? Does she have a nice house and stuff?"

Lily's face lit up. "It was *awesome*, Sar. I've never seen such a nice house. A movie theater in the basement! And maids—two, no, actually, *three* of them—serving us food on platters! I didn't get to meet her mom and dad, though. They were in New York City at some movie opening or something. But you wouldn't believe the food! There was this gooey-cheesy thing baked in a piecrust, and little hot dogs—the good ones, not the gross kind they serve in the cafeteria, and delicious homemade kettle corn! It was all so amazing. But it was also kind of weird to be sitting around talking about ways to help people who had lost all their stuff while eating all that delicious food."

I really wanted to ask about Mason. Whether he seemed legitimately upset that I wasn't there, or if he was hanging out with Jody all night. But hearing about the food was okay too, I guess.

"And actually, the auction is going to be awesome. Jody's dad knows the actor Jon Coddington, and he agreed to be the master of ceremonies!"

My eyes widened. Jon Coddington was a big movie star. Lily and I had seen a bunch of his movies.

"I didn't know he lived around here," I said.

"He doesn't. He lives in L.A. But I guess he's coming East for some reason next week, some event or something, so Jody's dad talked him into doing the auction."

I sighed. Another reason to wish I could go to the auction.

"So how was Mason?" I finally blurted out. "Was he hanging out with Jody all night?"

"Well, they *are* friends," said Lily, seeming to choose

her words carefully. "But I really think he was bummed that you weren't there."

Was she right? All I could think about was how pretty Jody was, and how cool her house was. What if Mason liked her? I mean, who could blame him?

"Calvin was so adorable," said Lily, sighing. "He's going to organize a bunch of guys to do yard cleanup for the storm victims."

"That's great," I said, and meant it.

"So the other reason I came over," said Lily, "aside from getting you up and out of bed, was that we all agreed to find cool stuff that people would want to bid on. And I thought that a session with Lady Azura would be awesome. Don't you think so?"

"I guess," I said. But I wasn't sure. I wondered if that was the sort of thing Lady Azura would agree to.

"I want to ask her to donate a spirit session. It'll be for the silent auction, not the live one, so she won't be embarrassed listening to people bidding on it—"

"Or not bidding on it," I added. "What if people don't bid?"

"Are you kidding? It will be a super-popular item! She's a mini celebrity now, after that piece appeared in the newspaper about her! Do you think you can help me talk her into it?"

I grinned. "I think she loves you so much you won't even need my help," I said. "But I'm in if you need me. I'll get dressed, and we can have breakfast and wait for her to come out."

Lily and I made pancakes, and then spent the morning quizzing each other on vocab for our *Julius Caesar* test on Monday.

At last Lady Azura emerged, and Lily pitched her idea to her. My great-grandmother pretended to be indifferent to the idea of donating her services to the auction, but I knew her well enough to know that she was excited about the idea. It was hard not to get excited about this auction. It sounded like it was going to be awesome. And if went off as well as everyone hoped, it was going to raise a lot of money.

I was still sorry I had to miss it, but I was glad my family was contributing in our own way.

Chapter 12

On Monday the weather turned cold and rainy, and I kept thinking about the people in Harbor Isle and some of the other nearby towns. Some of those people still didn't have electricity. I knew their homes must be getting cold. I hoped they had fireplaces and gas stoves.

At home I continued to search for Duggan every day, and he continued not to be anywhere.

At school the kids from Harbor Isle settled into the Stellamar routine. Mason and I were in the same math class, so it was fun to sit next to each other. But he didn't sit with me at lunch. The Harbor Isle kids had begun sitting together at their own tables—boys at one, girls at another. Jody and I weren't in any classes together, but Lily had her for Spanish and homeroom. Lily was now *convinced* that Jody wasn't as nice as she pretended to be. She claimed Jody barely said hello to her when other kids weren't around. I was still trying to give Jody the benefit of the doubt.

Friday after school, I hurried home to get ready for the wedding. At breakfast my dad had casually announced that it started at five, which surprised me, as I'd thought it would be much later. I hadn't even thought about what I was going to wear.

Up in my room, I took a quick shower, and then, still in my terry robe, with my hair coiled up in a towel turban, flung open my closet door to survey my options.

The best option was a dress I'd worn last year to the Harvest Dance. It had belonged to my mother. Would it still fit, though? I'd grown two inches taller since this time last year.

I slipped it over my head, feeling the silky-satin lining glide down my body like water. I realized with relief as I tugged up the zipper at the back that it still fit. Now it was shorter—a bona fide minidress, and maybe a little more snug-fitting than last year. But I had to admit, it still looked pretty nice on me.

Downstairs I heard my dad burst in through the

side door, no doubt frazzled from having had to leave the office early. I heard him thump up the stairs and into his room, and soon after that, his shower started.

I was slipping into my black flats when I heard a knock on the front door, and then Lily's voice calling to me from the front hallway.

"Lil!" I called, clattering down the front stairs. "What are you doing here? I thought you were at the auction!"

My dad came clumping down the stairs before Lily could respond. His curly hair was wet and coiled into ringlets like a poodle's, and he was trying to tie his tie while holding his nice shoes clamped against his side.

"Hey, Mr. Collins! And hello, gorgeous!" said Lily, looking admiringly at my outfit. "I just came by to tell Lady Azura that I'm headed to the auction early to set up, but my mom is coming to pick her up later on to take her there."

"Honey, we have to go," said my dad, hopping along the floor and trying to put on his shoes standing up. "This is a pretty low-key wedding, but we're going to be late."

"Go ahead to her room and tell Lady Azura," I said

to Lily, giving her a quick hug. "I think she's begun the elaborate process of getting herself ready for the evening. And have fun tonight."

Lily gave me a rueful smile and headed down the hallway toward Lady Azura's rooms.

As Dad and I drove off for the wedding, I tried not to think about how much I would rather be at the auction. But my dad looked so happy to be together. I put the thought out of my head and resolved to have fun.

And I did. The wedding was awesome.

It was all in one place—not a church first, like the other weddings I'd been to. It was more like a big party. The groom, Costi, was really handsome and friendly and gave me a big bear hug when my dad introduced me. I liked him immediately. And the bride was beautiful. Then there was really good food, and the live band played the kind of music that made you want to dance to it.

I was dancing the third dance in a row with my dad when suddenly I stopped dead and gaped over his shoulder.

He turned around to see what I was gaping at.

A famous movie star was standing near the food table, chatting away with a group of people.

My dad grinned. "I guess you've spotted Jon Coddington," he said. "Didn't I mention he was going to be here?"

I shook my head. Finally found words. "He's supposed to be the master of ceremonies at the auction tonight," I said. "What is he doing here?"

"He's actually a friend of both the bride and the groom. Costi introduced me to him once before, a few years ago. You want to meet him? Maybe he still remembers me."

Before I could answer, my dad had pulled me over to the group, which parted to let us approach.

It turned out Jon Coddington did remember my dad. Fondly, it seemed. He clapped him on the back and asked him how things were since the move to New Jersey. I couldn't believe that Jon Coddington knew who my dad was. While I was standing there with my mouth hanging open, he grinned at me and shook my hand. Then he turned to my dad. "She's beautiful, Mike!" he said. "Must take after her mom!"

The group laughed, as did my dad.

Jon Coddington had just called me beautiful. I'm surprised I didn't faint on the spot.

"So I hear you've double-booked yourself tonight, Jon," said my dad. "Sara tells me you're supposed to emcee the auction at her school later tonight."

"Oh! That's your school?" Jon said, turning to me. "Awesome! Will you be at the auction later, Sara?"

"Me? Well, um, no, I don't think so," I stammered out, looking at my dad for help.

"You have to go!" he said with a big grin. "There's plenty of time to get there. Besides, the auction can't start without me, right?"

Everyone laughed at this, too.

And then someone pulled Jon into another group of people, and my dad and I headed back to our table.

"You know what, kiddo? I'm really beat," said my dad, stifling a yawn. "Mind if we head home?"

"Sure, that's fine," I said, gathering up my jacket and bag.

"Why don't I drop you off at school on the way back?" he said. "Maybe you can check out the auction after all."

I narrowed my eyes at him. I knew he was leaving

early for my benefit. But I pretended to go along with it. "Sure," I said casually, like I didn't care one way or the other. "Sounds good."

As we pulled up at my school, I turned toward my dad. "Thanks, Daddy-o," I said softly.

"You're welcome, kiddo," he said, and then leaned over to try to maneuver around his seat belt to give me a hug.

I hugged him back and then stepped out of the car.

When I walked into the building, I could hear the murmur of the crowd coming from the gym. I hung up my coat on the rolling rack in the hallway outside the gym doors and stepped into the gym. It seemed as though the whole town had shown up for the event. Tables lined the outskirts in a U shape, with silent auction items placed on them where people could sign their names and their bids. There was a long table piled with stuff to eat and drink, and I could see Mrs. Randazzo and some other parents bustling around, selling people refreshments. Smaller, round tables had been set up in the interior. I spotted Lady Azura, dressed in a dazzling red sparkly dress, holding court at a table of older people. And then I spotted Lily and some of my other friends at a table close to the stage. I headed over.

"Sara!" squealed Lily, jumping up from the table. She threw her arms around me as though seeing me was the most exciting thing ever. Then, while she still had me clenched, she whispered into my ear.

"Mason saw you come in. He was totally staring. Don't look! He's still staring at you!"

I felt myself flush and stepped away. "Where's Calvin?" I asked, to change the subject.

"He's over there, tying balloons." She pointed toward a corner booth I hadn't yet noticed. There was Calvin and an older guy, and a long line of little kids. Calvin and the other guy were making balloon animals and silly balloon hats.

"Can you believe how talented he is?" said Lily. "Who knew the guy could make balloon animals?"

"He definitely has hidden depths," I agreed.

"He is just so awesome," she said. "And Sar, I'm beginning to think he might like me. *Like*-like me, I mean."

I squeezed her hand. "He'd be a dope not to," I said. "Has the auction started yet?"

"No! Jon Coddington got here about two minutes ago. It's not supposed to start until eight. Can you believe such a big star is actually here, in little old Stellamar, doing a fund-raiser?"

I started to tell Lily about how I had actually just met him, but Jody appeared out of nowhere and interrupted me.

"Sara! So glad you could make it," she said, but her tone lacked enthusiasm.

"Thanks," I said, feeling Lily step on my toe and trying to ignore her.

"So yeah, my dad arranged for Jon Coddington to be here. Pretty cool, huh? Maybe afterward I'll introduce you guys. I kind of promised the table I would, so—"

"Sara! You made it!" said a male voice behind me.

I turned. It was Jon Coddington. I heard Lily gasp next to me.

"Yeah, I decided to show up after all." I smiled at him.

He put a hand on my shoulder. "Guess what?" he asked, and then continued without waiting for me to guess. "I won Lady Azura's silent auction! She's going to do a session for me next time I come to New York. I am so psyched!"

"That's great," I said, genuinely delighted. I was also aware that Jody and Lily and the whole table full of my friends were all staring at me, dumbfounded. I don't usually like being the one people are staring at, but I was kind of enjoying this moment.

"Oops, better head on up to the stage. See you soon," he said, and hustled away.

Lily grabbed my arm. I looked at her and realized she was speechless.

Jody looked pretty stunned as well.

"Come on, guys," I said to them. "We'd better go sit down."

I sat down next to Lily. Mason and Calvin sat across from us, with Jody on Mason's other side. I could feel Mason's gaze rest on me from time to time, but I didn't meet his eye. I was too worried I'd blush.

The auction was a giant success. Jon Coddington was funny and charming and managed to get people to bid on stuff they might not otherwise have bid on, just with his infectious good humor. He poked gentle fun at some of the bidders, goading them to bid higher and higher—which they then did. He finished the last item and banged his gavel to deafening applause. Then he apologized for rushing out, but said he had a really early call time in the morning. Jody explained to the table that he wasn't talking about a phone call; it was acting lingo for the time he had to be on the set. The other kids seemed to be hanging on her every word.

As Lily and I stood near the coatrack, searching for our coats, Mason caught up with me.

"Hey," he said.

"Hey," I said, finally spotting my jacket and pulling it off the hanger.

"You have a ride home?"

"My dad said he'd come pick me up if I wanted him to," I said.

"Or maybe I could just walk you."

I felt a charge of electricity crackle through my body. "Um, okay," I said.

I shot Lily a look, and she nodded back at me and wiggled her eyebrows. I knew that was her way of saying I should definitely walk home with him. She headed over to where Calvin and Luke and Miranda were talking. We exchanged another look, which said we'd talk later.

I texted my dad quickly to tell him I was walking

home, and headed outside with Mason.

We walked in silence for a few steps. Two shy people. Not the best combination for conversation. Finally I thought of something to say.

"So I guess they raised a lot of money tonight."

"Yep."

The conversation languished again.

I tried again.

"How does Stellamar Middle compare to Harbor Isle in terms of the workload?"

He shrugged. "About the same," he said.

I kicked myself for bringing up school. I didn't even know if he liked school. Even though I knew a lot about him, there was also a lot I didn't know. I mean, I knew a lot about his special powers. And that he made my skin heat up like I had a fever, but I had no idea how he felt about things like homework and studying.

"So would you like to go out with me tomorrow night?" he blurted out suddenly.

"What?" I felt a jolt, like I'd been shocked. We stopped walking.

Then I tried again. "I mean, yes. Okay."

Mason's face broke into a huge grin, and I grinned

back. We stood there smiling at each other and then started walking again.

"So . . . what would you like to do?" Mason asked a few moments later. "A movie? Go out for pizza? Haunted house on the boardwalk?"

I laughed. I knew he was kidding about the last option. We'd been through the Midnight Manor on the boardwalk together last summer and had a pretty harrowing experience. I don't think either one of us really wanted to set foot in there again.

"Maybe pizza?" I said, thinking fast. Movies were nice and all, but it was hard to really talk during a movie. We could talk a lot over pizza. There was a lot I wanted to learn about Mason.

We reached my street and turned down toward my house. I was hoping somehow the street could grow longer, just so I'd have more time to walk alongside him. But in about thirty seconds we were standing in front of my house. On the lighted porch, I could see the outline of the knitting spirit who always sat on the swing.

"Okay, then," he said, and his green eyes darted a look at my face. He looked as nervous as I felt. He leaned toward me a little, and I went stock-still. Was he going to kiss me?

Instead he scooped up my hand and squeezed it with both of his. They were warm and strong. "I'll text you tomorrow and we can pick a time and place and all that. . . ."

"Okay."

He gave my hand one more squeeze, turned on his heel, and walked away.

I ran inside to call Lily.

Chapter 13

The next day, Saturday, Lily came over after breakfast. We'd spent an hour talking on the phone the night before. Evidently Calvin had walked her home, and he'd kissed her good night. A quick peck on the cheek, but still. He hadn't asked her out on a date like Mason had asked me, but we both figured that a good-night kiss definitely meant as much.

I wondered if Mason had gone home and called Cal and if they had spent time talking about us the way Lily and I had about them. I asked Lily, but she said boys probably didn't do stuff like that. At most they would have texted each other about it.

After we'd exhausted the topic of Mason and Cal, Lily brought up Duggan. I told her I still hadn't seen him, and that I was getting ready to give up.

"Sara, you cannot give up!" Lily said firmly. "I

won't let you. This is too important!"

"I know it's important, Lil . . . it's one of the most important things ever. But I can't *make* him appear. I tried that with Lady Azura, remember?"

"But you didn't try it with me," Lily said.

And then she talked me into her scheme.

So that's why when she arrived at my house this morning, she was carrying a big brown paper shopping bag. I knew what was inside it.

I followed her upstairs.

We went into the blue room. Out of habit, I looked in every corner for a sign of Duggan, but as usual, he wasn't there.

Lily went over to the bed and pulled out the box, placing it on the worn floral bedspread with special care. She climbed onto the bed and sat cross-legged, bouncing up and down a little with excitement.

I kicked off my sneakers and climbed onto the bed to sit opposite her, with the box in between us.

"I guess I'm as ready as I'll ever be," I said.

She'd convinced me to try to conjure Duggan with the spirit board. I was desperate enough to give it a try. I didn't think it was going to work, but Lily did.

And I had learned to trust Lily about stuff like this. Even though she couldn't see spirits like I could, she had what Lady Azura called "keen insight" into things. Maybe she knew something I didn't.

We took out the board and placed it across our knees.

"Okay," said Lily, unfolding the instructions. "Now we place our fingertips lightly but firmly, without pressure, on this thing, so as to allow it to move around easily. It's called a planchette; don't ask me why."

She held up a heart-shaped wooden thing supported by three small plastic feet. She put it on the board, and we lightly touched it with our fingertips.

"So now we ask a question and it's supposed to move all on its own, with no pushing from us, and spell out a message from the spirit."

"Open mind, open mind," I said to myself under my breath.

Lily looked at me, as though waiting for my cue. I shrugged a little. She frowned and looked down at our fingers on the planchette.

"Okay, here goes nothing," she said.

"Okeydoke," I said, feeling dubious.

"Mr. Duggan? We're really hoping you'll come see us. Sara and I? We're hoping you can come and talk with us. Hello?" asked Lily in a low voice.

We sat, staring down at our fingers resting gently on the movable part. I opened my mind. Allowed myself to listen, to look, to *feel* whether there was a spiritual presence in the room.

I didn't feel anything.

"Maybe I should start with something easier. Like a yes or no question," whispered Lily. "Mr. Duggan. Will you talk to us?"

A minute passed by. Then another. Then more. Outside I could hear it was starting to rain.

We sat in perfect silence for possibly five minutes. The old clock on the mantelpiece did not tick, the way it had in my dream. I supposed no one had wound it in years. Whatever dim hopes I may have had faded. Outside, the formerly sunny day had grown gray and rainy. So now it was dim and shadowy in the room. I was just about to call it off, to thank Lily for trying, when something happened. Something changed.

Ever so slightly, the room seemed to tilt and everything around me went blurry, like I was underwater all of a sudden. My heart started beating faster, and I could hear my breathing growing shallow. I knew what was happening. I was having a vision.

I squeezed my eyes shut for a moment, and when I opened them again, I saw myself in the room, just as I had been in my dreams. This time, instead of being seated at the desk, I was sitting cross-legged on the floor, writing in that same purple book. Once again, my hair was longer. And then a shadow moved behind me. But now whoever was casting the shadow emerged into the light, and I saw his face. It was Duggan.

The other me looked up from my writing, and my hair fell back from my face.

And then I realized it wasn't my face. The girl was not me at all. She looked almost exactly like me, but there were small differences. For one thing, she looked older. Older than I am now, older than she had looked in my dreams. She looked like me in a few years. But she wasn't me.

She was my mother.

"Duggan, I can't see you, but I am hoping you are here. You are here, aren't you?" She looked around the room. For a moment her gaze seemed to settle on Duggan, but I don't think she could see him. It reminded me of how Lady Azura acted during our séances. She could sense that spirits were there, but she would look right through them because she couldn't see them.

My mother's cheeks were flushed with excitement. I tried to tattoo the image of her face on my brain. Seeing her alive—hearing her talk—was amazing. Her voice sounded so much like my own.

"It was crazy, Duggan," the girl, my mother, Natalie, was saying. "She was my daughter! Or she will be my daughter in the future, after I grow up and get married. I *met* her. I talked to her in my dream. We talked about everything, and it all makes sense, even though it's so crazy!"

Duggan stood there, just listening. The expression on his face was kind.

"I'm going to write it all down in here. For her to find. So she knows everything." She looked up as if hoping to see Duggan. He was right there, but her gaze flicked by him. She went on. Her voice came out a whisper. "She told me her name was Sara. That's my favorite name, so it makes sense that would be her name, doesn't it?"

"Sara," Duggan echoed. "'Tis a fine name, I'll warrant."

And then the vision vanished. Suddenly. It was just over.

I searched around the room desperately, trying to bring the vision back. To hear more of what my mother had to say about me. She said we'd met. But where? When? Why didn't I remember any of this? Had it not happened yet?

I squeezed my eyes closed and prayed that when I opened them, I'd see my mother again. But the vision was over. It was just Lily and me on the bed.

I drew in a deep breath. I looked down. Focused on Lily, and the board between us. Beneath our fingers, the planchette began to move. I felt Lily tense up. Slowly it glided toward the upper left corner of the board. Toward the word "no."

Duggan had answered Lily's question, "Will you talk to us?" The answer was—

Almost at "no," the planchette suddenly swerved down and to the left and stopped over the letter *A*.

A?

Then it moved to *Y*.

Then to *E.*

"Aye." That meant yes.

I heard Lily draw a sharp breath.

She and I looked at each other, and her expression looked to me as wild and surprised as mine must have looked to her.

I turned my head slowly to look around the room. For a second, I thought I saw Duggan, over in a corner. But then I realized it was just an old coat hanging from a coatrack. My gaze traveled to the next corner, and the next.

And then I saw him.

My hands flew to my lap, my fists clenched in shock.

Lily could tell that I had seen something. She turned slowly to look in the direction of my gaze, but she couldn't see him. She turned back to me.

"Is he here, Sar?" she said in a barely audible voice.

"Yes."

"Then *talk* to him!" she hissed.

I pushed the board to the side and stood up, so that I was facing him.

He was dressed in his old blue coat and his battered

three-cornered hat. It was the right-aged Duggan, the old one who had told me about the message. He squinted at me beneath his fierce black brows, and it occurred to me that what seemed like gruffness might just have been that he was nearsighted. Maybe that was why he had passed by me in front of Scoops without saying anything. I remembered how kind he'd looked, listening to my mom talk about me. He was a good man, I decided. A friendly spirit. I believed he would help me.

"Hello, Mr. Duggan," I said, as calmly as I could so I wouldn't scare him away. "Thanks so much for coming back."

"The sea, 'tis the accomplice of human restlessness," he said, more to himself than to me.

"Sir?" I said.

He looked at me sharply, as though noticing me for the first time. "Dash my buttons, you resemble 'er, lass, I daresay!"

"Natalie, you mean?" I asked eagerly. "Yes, I've been told that. Natalie was my mother. I believe you knew her, sir?"

"Aye, and a cleverer lass with a pen and paper than

ever I clapped eyes upon," he said. "Never learned to read and write very well myself. But the lass was smart as paint! And hark ye: The lass could draw pictures, the likeness of which I had ne'er before seen, I'll lay to that."

He knew my mom, I realized, my heart swelling. He really knew her.

"Please, Mr. Duggan," I said, trying hard not to appear as desperately eager as I felt. I didn't want to alarm him. "You mentioned something about a message from Natalie. Did she—do you know where I might be able to find it?"

Suddenly there was a clap of thunder, which made me jump. Lily gave a tiny squeak, so she must have been as startled as I. Rain streamed down the window.

Duggan turned toward the window and furrowed his brow. "Heavy weather afoot," he said. "Must be sure all is shipshape and seaworthy."

I remembered how Lady Azura had said he tended to appear just before storms. But was he beginning to fade? *No! Not yet!* I screamed on the inside.

"Please, don't go," I begged. "They predicted a few passing showers today, but it's not like it's going to turn into another big storm or anything. You don't need to check on your ships just yet. Please, can you tell me where to find the message from Natalie? She spoke of meeting me, but I don't remember any of it. I need to find the message she left for me. Can you help me? "

"Aye," he said, nodding, but his voice was fainter, and I could see directly through his shimmery image to the coatrack behind him. "'Tis in the cupboard. Look ye under the boards."

"Which cupboard?" I asked. "In this room? Or somewhere—"

I stopped talking midsentence. It was no use. He was gone.

Chapter 14

I turned to look at Lily. Her eyes were huge.

"Did you see him?" I asked.

She shook her head so hard her chandelier earrings swayed. She hadn't been able to see him. But from the look on her face, I knew she believed that he had been here.

"What did he say? Did he know your mom when she was younger? And I heard you say something about your mom meeting you? And a cupboard?"

I nodded. Kept nodding. "We have to look for something under some boards. And I think—I'm pretty sure—what we're looking for is a purple journal. She met me, Lily. I'm not sure—maybe in a dream—but she wrote about it and left it for me to find. I think maybe she left instructions for me on how to reach her. . . ."

My voice trembled with excitement.

Lily hopped up, ready to take charge. "Okay, so let's look. Should we start with the cupboards in the kitchen? Or maybe the pantry cupboards?"

I clutched my arms against the sudden chill in the room, thinking hard. "I think 'cupboard' is an old term for 'closet.' And I remember Lady Azura complaining about how few closets there were in the house, considering the number of rooms. She told me that the Victorians didn't build closets. They had those big, freestanding wardrobes instead, like that one over there." I pointed at the massive old wardrobe across the room. "Or they hung their clothes on pegs or stuck them into trunks."

"Okay," said Lily, tapping her foot impatiently. She was eager to start searching. But I knew we had to be smart about it. This was a big old house. We'd be searching for days if we didn't stop and think for a moment.

"There are *some* closets in the house," I continued. "I think they were built later, after the house had been around for a while. But definitely they would have existed while my mom was alive."

"Makes sense," said Lily. "So where should we

start?" She looked around the room. "There isn't a closet in here," she said.

"We could start at the top and work our way down," I proposed. That sounded like as good a plan as any.

So we did. After scurrying down to my father's workbench in the basement to dig out two flashlights, we headed back up, all the way to the attic. But aside from a small storage area under the eaves, there weren't any actual closets up there. On the third floor, we had to release Henry, the little-boy spirit who inhabited my craft closet.

"We just need to look in the closet for a second, Henry," I explained to him. He was delighted to run free around my craft room. I eyed my canisters of colored pencils and paintbrushes near my art table, knowing they posed a serious temptation to the mischievous little squirt. "Be good," I said. "And I'll ask Lily here to bring Buddy over to play with you tomorrow."

Henry loved Lily's dog, Buddy. He nodded eagerly and then sat in the corner, his hands folded in his little lap.

But I still didn't trust him. I had Lily sit with her back against the open door to prevent Henry from locking us in. I'd learned that lesson already. But there was no loose floorboard in my crafts closet.

After luring Henry back into the closet, we headed downstairs and into my room to look. Nothing in there. Then we checked my dad's room, and finally the pink bedroom, where the spirit of the woman in the rocking chair observed us without commenting. That room didn't even have a closet.

"Should we check in there again?" asked Lily, pointing to the blue bedroom.

"No point," I said. "There aren't any closets. Let's check the downstairs."

We checked the coat closet near the front door. We checked the cupboard under the front stairs, the one with the triangular door. We checked the cupboards in the pantry, and even the kitchen cupboards, although I was sure we wouldn't find anything. There was no closet in Lady Azura's séance room, which was a good thing, because she had a client in there. I didn't bother with her bedroom, because why would my mother hide her diary in there?

We returned to the blue bedroom and sat on the bed side by side. I fought back tears of frustration.

"Is he just messing around with me?" I asked. "Why would Duggan say that if it weren't true? He's kind of gruff, but he doesn't seem to be a malicious spirit."

Lily propped her chin on her hand and nodded glumly.

"She was talking about me like she met me in a vision or a dream or something. But how come I don't remember? I have all these other dreams and visions and I always remember them, but—"

Suddenly I felt Lily sit up straight. Her fingers squeezed my arm.

"Ow! What?"

Wordlessly, she pointed across the room. I followed her gaze.

At first I saw nothing. And then I saw it.

Half obscured by the battered old wardrobe, and only a few feet high, was a door. It was flush with the wall, and covered by the faded blue wallpaper, but you could see that it had been cut into the wall, and that it was definitely a door.

We looked at each other. We both hopped off the bed and moved across the room like we were part of a choreographed dance. We both crouched down to look. The door was one of those old, hidden things with a spring on the inside. You can just push it in and it pops out and opens.

"Help me move this wardrobe," I said to her.

It wouldn't budge.

We had to open it up and lug the hangers full of old coats out of it, piling them onto the bed. I guessed they must have belonged to Lady Azura's husband, my great-grandfather, because they felt like heavy men's overcoats. Then we pulled out the four heavy drawers, which had nothing in them, except some old sachets that had lost their scent, and stacked them carefully to one side.

Once again, we stood up and tried to move it with all our collective strength. Slowly, slowly, it began to budge from the wall. We managed to get it far enough away so that the angle would allow the little door to open.

"Should we?" I whispered to her, my heart pounding.

"Go for it," she said. "You do it, Sar. I'll shine my flashlight for you."

I pushed on the door.

With a tiny, audible unlatching sound, it sprang open, revealing a dark, dusty interior.

Lily fumbled with her flashlight, her hands shaking with excitement, and finally managed to turn it on and point it into the closet. We both peered inside.

Almost at the same time, we both sneezed. There was a good half an inch of dust inside.

It was a small, rectangular interior, maybe two feet across and three feet deep. Big enough to stash a small trunk, maybe. There was nothing in it but an old, sprung mousetrap. I was grateful it didn't contain a dead mouse.

To the left, near the roughly plastered wall, two of the floorboards were definitely sticking up above the others. The old nails had worked their way out.

I looked at Lily. She looked at me, her eyes shining.

I reached in and gave them a tug. They lifted easily.

Lily shone the light beneath them. There was a purple book, just like the one I'd seen in my dreams. It was stashed inside a zipped-up plastic bag.

With shaking hands, I lifted it out and looked at Lily.

"This is the message," I said in a whisper. "From my mother."

About the Author

Phoebe Rivers had a brush with the paranormal when she was thirteen years old, and ever since then she has been fascinated by people who see spirits and can communicate with them. In addition to her intrigue with all things paranormal, Phoebe also loves cats, French cuisine, and writing stories. She has written dozens of books for children of all ages and is thrilled to now be exploring Sara's paranormal world.

Want to know what happens to Sara next?

Here's a sneak peek at the next book in the series:

Yesterday and Today

Alone at last.

Upstairs in my room, I sat on the floor next to my bed. My hands shook a little as I stared down at the diary. My mother's diary. My mother, who I had never met because she died giving birth to me. Now I held in my hands the diary she kept when she was my age. I was finally going to "meet" her . . . at least, sort of.

Earlier in the day, my best friend, Lily, and I had found the diary hidden in a secret closet in a room I usually refer to as the blue bedroom because of the blue walls in there. But now Lily had gone home. She'd known without me having to tell her that I wanted to be alone with my mom's diary. I shared just about everything with Lily, but this was different.

I set it down gently in my lap. Brushed it lightly with my fingertips. Took a deep breath.

"Whatcha got there?" demanded a loud voice in my doorway.

I whirled around to see who it was. Could it be my mother?

It *was* a spirit. But not my mother's.

Perhaps I should explain. I can see spirits. People who have died. I've been able to see them for as long as I can remember. The house I live in is filled with spirits. The old Victorian house in Stellamar, New Jersey, which belonged to my great-grandmother, Lady Azura. My dad and I had moved here two summers ago. At first I didn't know that Lady Azura was my great-grandmother. I'd just thought she was some kooky lady who told fortunes and read tea leaves. She was one of several secrets that had been kept from me for a long time. But I'd grown to love Lady Azura, and by the time I found out she was my great-grandmother, I was thrilled about it.

The spirit standing in my doorway wasn't one I was familiar with. Not one of our regulars, as I had come to think of them. We had several that inhabited the house, and I knew them all. This was an older woman. She had a lot of makeup on, and her hair was all done up like she'd just stepped out of the salon.

I slipped the diary off my lap and nudged it under my bed. Then I stood up and walked over to her.

"Can I help you with something?" I asked, trying to be polite when in reality I was really annoyed by the interruption.

She wandered into my room, checking out my stuff. I bristled as her semitransparent hands touched my things.

"Don't suppose so." She shrugged, examining the photo of my mom on my bedside table. "I was just bored. Name's Shirley. My son, Harry, and his wife are downstairs. They're trying to get me to show up and tell them where I hid my will. I think that's all they care about. And I'll tell them. But in my own sweet time." She laughed mischievously. "It's much more interesting up here."

That explained it, then. My great-grandmother was a fortune-teller. She could conjure spirits. People flocked here for her services.

Lady Azura must be holding a séance with clients downstairs. She must have summoned this spirit for them. I had to get rid of her. Politely, of course.

"Thanks so much for dropping in," I said. "I am sure Harry and his wife can't wait for you to appear to them, though."

"Pah!" she said, waving her hand. "I doubt it. He's a good boy, my Harry. Not sure what he was thinking marrying That Girl, but then, he didn't exactly consult me before he popped the question." Her voice got lower as she started fiddling with my camera. I think maybe she was getting a little emotional. "I did notice that his wife was wearing my butterfly pin. It's an old thing, probably not worth very much anymore. I guess Harry gave it to her after I died. I heard her tell the fortune-teller that it belonged to me and how happy she was to have it. It sort of seemed like she meant it . . . but I think she must think it's valuable and that's why she likes it."

"Actually, I don't think that's true. I can sense that Harry and his wife want you to show yourself. I think they really miss you." To be honest, I wasn't getting much of a vibe from downstairs at all, but I was still pretty sure that what I said was true. And she seemed pleased to hear it. I had learned from Lady Azura that spirits really aren't all that different from the living.

They hold grudges and make mistakes just like people do. Sometimes they just need to be set on the right track. "I sense that they're waiting for you, Shirley, and that you must be very important to both of them or else they wouldn't be here."

She stood up, tugging at her dress and patting her hair. "You can sense all that? Do you have the gift, like the lady downstairs?"

"Well, I am her great-granddaughter," I replied. Even I could hear the pride in my voice when I said it.

Shirley regarded me carefully for a moment or two, as if she was trying to make up her mind about me. "All right, then," she said finally. "I shall go join them." And she shimmered into nothingness.

I waited a minute more. I didn't want to be interrupted again. But my room was quiet. I sat down and pulled the diary out from under my bed.

It was purple, with a puffy kind of cover, sort of like a photo album. Slightly scuffed in places. The word DIARY, embossed in gold lettering, was the only thing on the cover. The corners were bent in a little, as though it had been dropped once or twice.

I took a few deep breaths and tried to calm my

racing nerves. This was my first real glimpse into my mother's life, her world. I'd been so eager to meet her, but her spirit hadn't shown itself to me. I'd found out about the diary from another spirit, that of an old sailor named Duggan. Duggan was one of our regulars, and when he was here, he was usually in the blue bedroom. He'd told me about the diary. And then I'd dreamed about where it was hidden. Only Lily and I knew about the diary. I hadn't told my dad or Lady Azura about it. Yet. For now, I wanted it to be my secret. Something I shared with my mother. Just the two of us.

With a trembling hand, I opened to the first page.

Girlish handwriting. Purple ink. Fat, loopy letters. The first entry was dated August 7, 1984.

She would have just turned twelve. The age I was when I first moved to Stellamar. She'd probably received the diary for her twelfth birthday.

A thought struck me. What if she only wrote in the diary for a few days or weeks and then got bored and forgot all about it? That would be really disappointing. But then again, I guessed a small glimpse into my mom's life was better than nothing.

I fanned the pages. There was a lot of writing. She'd stuck with it. The entries came to a stop about two-thirds of the way through the book. Some days had short entries, just a sentence or two. Other days went several pages, the writing growing more urgent and slanted, as though she'd written while upset or excited. I resisted the urge to read these more interesting-looking entries. I'd start from the beginning and read it all in order. I turned back to the first page.

And then my phone vibrated, telling me I had a text.

In exasperation, I pulled my phone from my back pocket. I was going to shut it off, something I almost never ever did, but I didn't want to be interrupted. Then I noticed who the text was from: Lily.

SORRY. I KNOW YOU'RE BUSY WITH YOU KNOW WHAT. BUT PLEASE CALL ME ASAP. IT'S MUCHO IMPORTANT!

I quickly texted back.

OK. WILL CALL SOON.

Then I turned off my phone.

I looked down at the diary. I couldn't wait to meet her. My mom. Natalie, as she was known to everyone else.

I read the first line . . .

Dear Diary,

. . . and then everything got a little blurry and I was plunged into a vision.

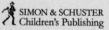
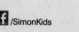